Growing Up
Can Be Difficult

By: <u>Captain Sean</u>

All Stories Written by – Captain Sean
Stories Managed by – Captain Sean Productions

ISBN: 978-1-329-01130-4

Table of Contents

Chapter 1 – Leena

Scene 1

-In a seemingly ordinary high school library, a teenage boy named Jimmy is writing over a piece of notebook paper. Suddenly Jimmy's laid-back but loyal friend Peter comes in interested in what Jimmy is doing.

Peter – Well if it ain't my super brainy (but still remains cool in my book) best friend Jimmy. Whatcha working on there?

Jimmy – Doodling.

-Peter then holds up a paper full of very complex mathematical equations.

Peter – This is doodling?

Jimmy – I sometimes do it to get my mind flowing. My mind can move pretty quickly remember. Sometimes I develop awesome new ideas by just letting my mind free flow.

-Peter gives the paper back to Jimmy.

Peter – Right. You do math equations, I'll watch TV, and then we'll all feel relaxed.

-From a nearby door, a girl comes in carrying her books but her head is tilted a bit sideways and her face appears stuck in some form of partial smile. The girl makes a bigger smile as she sees Jimmy and waves to him.

Jimmy – Oh, hey Leena.

Leena – Hiiiiiii.

-Leena's only spoken word is a bit drawn out as she slowly walks to a place to sit down.

Peter – Hey. What's up with that girl? She don't look right and walks kinda weird.

Jimmy – She's just different Peter.

Peter – But not different like you.

Jimmy – Yeah, thank you for pointing that out. But getting to the point, Leena has a special type of mental disability. Her brain doesn't process information like the rest of us do and has some problems with coordination. She's part of the special education program here. While most students in the program get to be included in some of the normal classes here, she requires a lot of specialized attention. She can however make it on her own to the library.

Peter – Man. That's a rough lifestyle it sounds like she's leading. Hasn't anyone out there made any kind of medicine to cure people of stuff like that yet?

Jimmy – Unfortunately, no. Aside from becoming involved in the special education field, there isn't much that can be done for her except pray.

Peter – Well that sounds like something cool to put at the top of my prayer list tonight. See ya.

-Peter walks away. Jimmy then goes back to his paper full of math equations and pauses as he takes a closer look at them.

Jimmy – Hmm. I wonder...

Scene 2

-In the high school cafeteria Jimmy is sitting in front of Leena while writing incredibly fast. Leena notices this.

Leena - You... write... faaast.

-Jimmy only briefly looks at Leena as he smiles.

Jimmy – Thanks for noticing.

-Nearby Peter is leading two girls named Monica and Kaitlyn who both have notepads and other items with them that hint that they are young high school newspaper reporters.

Monica - Where are we going Peter?

Kaitlyn - Yeah. When we said that we were low on school newspaper material and you said you had an interesting story, I thought it would be something big. You better not be playing some kind of trick on us.

Peter - It may not be the kind of big thing you're into but it can be.

-Peter then stops right next to where Leena is sitting.

Peter – Monica, Kaitlyn, this is Leena. Leena, these are my friends.

-Monica and Kaitlyn wave slightly as a smiling Leena waves back.

Leena - H... Hii.

-Monica and Kaitlyn wave slightly as a skeptical looking Monica looks at Peter.

Monica – This is your idea for a newspaper story?

Peter – Hey, it's something.

Kaitlyn - So... Leena.... What are you into?

Leena - I... I.... need... help with...

-Leena holds out a straw with wrapping still on it. Peter takes the straw from Leena.

Peter - I'll help you out there.

-Peter takes the wrapping off the straw and puts the straw into a small carton of milk for Leena.

Peter - Here you go.

Leena - Thhhhhank you.

-Peter looks at Monica and Kaitlyn with smiles while Monica and Kaitlyn can only stand with skeptical looks on their faces.

Scene 3

-Peter and Jimmy are walking down a sidewalk while Jimmy is still writing quickly all over a notepad.

Peter - Man. All that prefix stuff in English in just crazy. What do you think Jimmy?

-Jimmy is barely looking at Peter.

Jimmy - It's an important function in the English language.

Peter – Whatever. So.... You were a bit quiet when we were eating lunch with Leena. You know once you spend some time with her she's not so bad. What do you think?

-Jimmy suddenly stops in his tracks with an amazed look on his face.

Jimmy - I think I've done it.

Peter - Done what?

Jimmy - It was a bit complicated. Even for me, but I've got it.

Peter - Got what Jimmy?

Jimmy - A special way of accomplishing it.

Peter- What?

Jimmy - A cure for mental disabilities.

Peter - A cure. For what kind?

Jimmy - All of them. It just took several dozen equations on brain structure. Pete... with this information I've developed, I can help all kinds of people with problems in thought processing and comprehension think correctly.

Peter - Jimmy. We already have ways to help like that. You were telling me about it the other day. Early intervention, classroom aids, support groups, special individualized curriculums for them...

Jimmy - But those are just ways to help those kind of people cope with what they have. Even though there are medications that help, no one's actually developed a cure that simply makes mental disorders disappear. I think I can do it.

Peter - Jimmy. This isn't like making a new satellite dish. This is about changing the human brain.

Jimmy - Changing the human brain for the better. Pete, I don't want to turn the human race into a bunch of super human geniuses. I just want to use my abilities to really help people. Pete, so many geniuses out there use their skills to just advance their own careers or make money. Very few of them literally put their entire mind into supporting those in need. However I am now.

-Peter sighs with a reluctant look on his face.

Peter - All right. I have no idea how you're gonna do it, but you go do it.

Scene 4

-In a living room, Jimmy sits in front of Leena's father and mother. The two parents both looked a bit stunned at what Jimmy has just explained to them.

Leena's Father – You want to do what to my daughter?

Jimmy - Cure her of her mental disability Mister and Mrs. Robins.

Leena's Mother - But how?

Jimmy - I've created a device that can make the synapses in Leena's brain access each other more appropriately. If this works she'll be able to talk and think like you've always wanted her to.

Leena's Father – How could you have made this? The type of device you're talking about has never been made by any scientist before. How can we be sure a device made by some high school student would?

Jimmy – Look, I understand I'm asking to do something that seems impossible. Something that would be deemed even illegal due to a lack of testing. However I'm somebody that's trying to improve the world here and now; not take my time in order to please the people at the top that are living comfortably. Like your daughter I am different. But I think I can use my differences to help Leena overcome hers. Please, I am only trying to help Leena. That's it.

-Leena's parents look at each other silently for a moment.

Leena's Father – All right. You have our approval to do what you want.

Jimmy - Thank you.

Scene 5

-In a small laboratory Leena sits in an easy chair as Jimmy is attaching a sophisticated type of head gear complete with many wires to Leena's head.

Leena – The chair... very soft.

Jimmy - All right Leena. I'm going to attach these wires to your head. I'm actually not quite sure of what you'll feel when this begins but please... try to understand I'm here to help you.

Leena – Heeeeelp?

Jimmy – Yeah. That's what I'm here to do.

-Jimmy then goes over to a control panel near him.

Jimmy - Okay. Everything's all hooked up. Ready to activate... now!

-Jimmy presses a button and then a quick bright light goes throughout the whole machine and Leena. Within seconds, it is over. Jimmy goes over and unhooks Leena from the machine.

Jimmy - Leena. How do you feel?

-Leena slowly looks at Jimmy.

Leena - I... feeeeel... good. Feel good.

-Jimmy has a sudden look of disappointment on his face.

Scene 6

-Peter and Jimmy are walking down a sidewalk together as Jimmy is going through pages of notes as he walks.

Jimmy - I don't understand where I went wrong Pete. I had all of the right formulas.

Peter – Sorry to hear about it man. So where's Leena?

Jimmy - I took her back to her house. I still don't get it though. Everything went together and added up.

Peter – Jimmy. You invented the procedure in less than two weeks. The kind of change you're hoping for just doesn't work that fast.

Jimmy – I guess you're right.

-Suddenly from around a corner Leena appears walking normally but her head is still slightly tilted to the side. Peter and Jimmy are surprised at Leena and run over to her.

Jimmy – Leena? What are you doing out here?

Leena – I... wanted to see you. So I... left my home and... found you. Now I'm starting to talk right. Jimmy. I can talk right. I can talk.

-An excited Jimmy puts his hands on Leena's shoulders.

Jimmy - Leena. You're talking faster and in full sentences.

-An excited looking Leena looks at the surroundings around her.

Leena - The sky is a shade of... light blue. The grass over there is dark green. The pavement is somewhat gray. Your eyes are a smooth shade of black.

Jimmy - That's right.

-Leena then begins to point all around her.

Leena – The bricks on that house are red. The grass over there should be mowed. That building is 7 stories tall and...

-Leena then stops to look closely at her arms.

Leena - My hands and arms. I've never felt such strong control over them before.

-Leena then looks right at Jimmy's face.

Leena - You helped me change. You helped me... become a better person.

Jimmy - I guess that's how you could refer to it.

Leena - There's so much to do. So much to say.

Jimmy - Hey. Why don't you re-explore the world by hanging out with me?

Leena - I'd like that.

Scene 7

-In the same laboratory from earlier Leena is sitting in a chair while Jimmy waves a scanner device over her.

Jimmy - It looks like all of my calculations were right on. It just took a while to set in.

Leena - Those are some pretty technical instruments you've acquired Jimmy.

Jimmy - How would you know?

Leena - Even though I never really responded to everything I heard, I still heard it. Even though it didn't seem like I understood it, a part of me took in everything I was exposed to. It was just getting my mind to link point A to point B that made it so difficult.

Jimmy - Incredible. Leena, your brain has not only been restructured to function correctly but it can also look back on your own memories and assess how you were thinking then.

Leena - That remark would be accurate.

Jimmy – Amazing.

Scene 8

-Jimmy and Leena are both sitting in a fast food restaurant together eating cheeseburgers.

Leena - Mmm. I know this stuff is fattening but it tastes so good.

Jimmy – I hear that.

Monica's Voice – Hey guys.

-The three turn their heads and see Monica and Kaitlyn walking over to the two.

Jimmy - Hey there ladies.

Leena - Hello there. How are you all doing?

-Monica and Kaitlyn's faces quickly go into shocked looks.

Kaitlyn - Fine. Leena. You're... sort of...

Leena - Talking and moving normal now? It's all right to point out.

Monica – But... how?

-Jimmy is now looking a bit nervous.

Jimmy - Well... umm... you see that...

Leena - You see there's this experimental new drug they're working on people like me. The first test has just been accomplished on me and Jimmy's here to help me get adjusted to normal life correctly.

Jimmy – Uh... yes. That's right.

Kaitlyn - Well this is interesting news.

Monica – Yeah it is. Now this could be good material for the school paper.

Jimmy - Well could you girls keep this under wraps for awhile? It is an experimental thing.

Kaitlyn – Oh, it's cool. But we want an exclusive as soon as possible.

Leena - You can count on it.

Monica - Thanks. Well we hope to talk to you later. See ya.

-Monica and Kaitlyn then walk away

Jimmy - Thanks for covering for me. But how did...

Leena – Examined your facial expressions and figured you wanted to keep your procedure under wraps.

Jimmy – To understand so much about a person just by looking at their face... Fascinating! I'd like to hear more about how you examine the world.

Leena – I'd like to as well but I should be getting home. My parents are going to be amazed by this. Hey, I know. Tomorrow let's have a picnic in the park together.

Jimmy - A picnic?

Leena - Yeah. You set it up for us and I'll give you any scientific insight on me you need.

Jimmy - Well what kind of smart dude would pass up a chance like that?

Leena - Sounds great. Tomorrow at ten then. See ya.

-A happy looking Leena walks out the restaurant as a happy looking Jimmy watches her.

Scene 9

-In his laboratory Jimmy has a joyous look on his face as he sits in front of Peter.

Jimmy - It was amazing Peter. All her life Leena couldn't move around normally and had limited communication. However now she can move and talk just like any person should. In fact I think she has a unique insight that no other person in the world has ever had before.

Peter – What do you mean by unique insight?

Jimmy - She has full recollection of what it was like to be mentally challenged. She can look back at her memories and accurately say what it was like. It's a little hard for even me to understand so I'm looking forward to talking about it with her more tomorrow.

Peter - I don't know Jimmy. She's never done this much talking in her life before. Are you sure all this talking is good for her.

Jimmy – Pete, she's been waiting to say so much all her life.

Peter - What about the scans you did on Leena earlier. Shouldn't you look at them in more detail? I mean after Leena's change you've barely looked at them.

Jimmy - I will tomorrow with Leena.

Peter – With Leena?

Jimmy – Pete, I think she is smarter then she seems. Well I better get ready for the picnic tomorrow.

Peter – Picnic? Since when do you do picnics?

Scene 10

-Jimmy sets up a blanket in the middle of a wide grassy area in a park and then hears Leena running over to him.

Leena – Jimmy!

-Leena then runs over to Jimmy and hugs him. Jimmy hugs her back and then lets her go.

Leena – I've always wanted to run up to a friend and hug them like that.

Jimmy – Wow. So... shall we eat?

Leena – We shall.

-Jimmy and Leena then both sit down next to each other as they begin to open up their basket.

Jimmy - I actually had to buy this last night.

Leena - Well it's very traditional looking.

-Leena then takes out a bag of candy corn.

Jimmy - I know. It's not all traditional.

-Leena puts the candy corn bag down with a big smile.

Leena - It's perfect.

Jimmy – So... how are things at home?

Leena - Great. I've never seen my parents so thrilled before. It's also been kind of weird.

Jimmy - Weird? Weird in what way?

-Leena then begins to stare at the grass.

Leena – Jimmy... when you look at the grass you just see grass... but when I used to look at it, it was so much more. When I was different it was strange compared to the way I see things now. I would look at things in a detail, in a way different then you probably would. On a day I could relax I would just look at things in my room or outside my house. I just looked at it. I would just pay attention to all of the detail around me. Sometimes it seemed like there was too much detail for me to look at it, but apparently I wasn't paying enough attention.

-Jimmy begins to scoot closer to Leena.

Jimmy - What do you mean?

Leena - Jimmy. My whole life I've lived with this... problem in me. I know my parents and teachers always said I wasn't, but at so many times it seemed like I was stupid. There I was stuck on some paper every other student had finished what seemed like hours ago.

Jimmy - It's hard for me to imagine what that would be like.

Leena - Basically everything I did in my life was hard. I could see the assignment. I knew what I had to do to accomplish it but... I had so much trouble doing it. I would try so hard to get to the end of something. So many times I would accomplish something wrong though. People helped me so much and so many of them had good intentions but I knew I was a burden on them. There were so many things I couldn't do on my own. I always needed somebody's help. And as nice as you and some of the other people were, there were always those who would say such terrible things to me. The awful names, the terrible things they would assume about my family members. It hurt so much... but the worst part was it was so difficult to say anything to defend myself. And when I tried, I would just say something else so stupid. I hated my life so much, but even if I wanted to end it I didn't even know how.

Jimmy - What kept you going?

Leena – Just having good people around me like you. You made me feel like I could actually do something with my life one day. Now I really can.

Jimmy – Well I'm glad I was able to help.

-Leena then scoots very close to Jimmy.

Leena - Jimmy. What if when I start going back to school some people make fun of me even more? What if they start calling me some kind of freak? What if some people think I was just faking my condition? What if...

Jimmy - Leena. There are some very sick people in the world that will make fun of someone based off anything. Whether you have a mental disability or just some mismatched socks, someone is going to try to find some way to make fun of you. You've just gotta hang in there and remember you're more important than those people will ever realize. And hey... you're important to me.

-Jimmy and Leena suddenly are left looking right at the other silently for several moments.

Leena – Thank you Jimmy.

Scene 11

-Peter and Jimmy are walking down the sidewalk together again.

Jimmy – We spent hours talking together Pete. Her insight on what her life was like when she had her condition, the way she looked at the specific attributes of things in life. Pete, she looked at life in a completely different way. Once she starts going back to school she could have the potential to become a real genius in no time. With my kind of intelligence and her type of unique insight we could do great things together.

Peter – So you believe she's actually a genius and want to do "work" with her. You like her don't you?

-Jimmy is now looking slightly embarrassed.

Jimmy – I do.

Suddenly Jimmy's cell phone rings and he turns it on.

Jimmy - Hello?

Leena's Voice - Jimmy. Can you please... come over to my house... now. Please.

Jimmy - Sure. I'm on my way.

Scene 12

-Leena is sitting on the bed of her bedroom with a very troubled look on her face. Jimmy enters the room with a smile.

Jimmy – Hey Leena.

-Leena turns her head slowly to look at Jimmy.

Leena - Jimmy... hi.

-Jimmy sits next to Leena.

Jimmy - Hey. Is something wrong?

Leena - Yes. Ever since an hour ago... I've started to... feel different again.

Jimmy - What do you mean?

Leena - I'm... not sure. It was taking me longer to do some things. Couldn't... concentrate right. My hands are even... starting to feel not right again.

-Jimmy is now looking more concerned while Leena then turns to look right at Jimmy with a very scared look on her face.

Leena - Jimmy. I'm starting to... become what I was before.

Jimmy – What!?

-Tears begin to go down Leena's face.

Leena - Everything is becoming more... confusing. Can't think right. I'm scared Jimmy. Very scared. I want to be... normal. Just want to be... normal.

-Jimmy puts his hands on Leena's shoulders.

Jimmy - Leena. Just try to hang in there and concentrate.

Leena - I... can't. I'm just... worried you won't like me... anymore.

Jimmy - Leena. There's nothing that'll change my feelings about you.

-Leena then begins to lean her body on Jimmy.

Leena - Don't leave... Jimmy.

-Jimmy then hugs Leena.

Jimmy - Don't worry Leena. I won't leave you. I won't leave you.

Scene 13

-In his laboratory Jimmy is starring at a computer screen as Peter walks in.

Peter - Have you figured out what happened?

-Jimmy slowly turns to look at Peter with a sad look on his face.

Jimmy - Yeah. I was just too excited to see it earlier. The changes I made in Leena's brain were practically artificial. And in this case, artificial changes also mean only temporary changes.

Peter - Could you do it again but make it more permanent?

-A frustrated Jimmy bangs his fist next to his computer.

Jimmy - No. According to my calculations if it's done again it could cause her to suffer major brain damage. From what I can see, there's no cure for mental disabilities. And if I can't create a cure then there's no hope for this problem at all.

Peter – Hold on. If you can't do it, then all hope is lost? There is something really wrong with your realization.

Jimmy – What do you mean?

Peter – Jimmy, I've noticed that during this whole ordeal you've only been depending on your own insights and assumed only *you* could solve this major issue. But don't you remember when you came to church with me that one time, you heard that sermon about when things are out of our control we need to have faith that God will take care of the rest. I mean didn't you pray at all during these last few days over Leena?

Jimmy – I… didn't.

Peter – Jimmy, I want a cure for all types of disabilities. But once I've done my part, I have to put the rest in Gods' hands, and also believe that he's gonna use these disabilities in some way for good. And… that's all I've gotta say for now. You're the smart one. I'm sure you'll figure the rest out.

-Peter then walks out of the laboratory. Jimmy then gets up and bangs his fist against the wall but then calms down as he begins to think hard.

Jimmy – For God so loved the world that he gave his only son. I guess even you Lord knows what it's like to see someone close to you suffer.

Scene 14

-In a school newspaper office Jimmy stands in front of Monica and Kaitlyn with a newspaper that has Leena's picture on it.

Jimmy - You made an article about Leena.

Monica - Yeah. We felt like we should.

Jimmy - But you didn't make it about her temporary recovery.

Kaitlyn - Well, we thought it would make a better article if we wrote about the struggles that people with mental disabilities go through.

-Jimmy folds up the newspaper and makes a brief smile.

Jimmy - It was a good article.

-Jimmy then leaves the school newspaper office and immediately sees Leena walking in an abstract way while carrying books. Jimmy watches Leena silently for a moment but then says to himself...

Jimmy – Hmm. I think there is something I can do to help Leena.

-Jimmy then immediately runs up to Leena with a friendly smile on his face.

Jimmy – Hey Leena. You need a friend to hang out with?

THE END

Chapter 2 – Future Unknown

Scene 1

-Outside of a high school laboratory, a male teenager named Keno is walking towards the laboratory door. His face is that of a slightly depressed young man as he knocks on the door.

Keno - Jimmy, are you in there?

-Suddenly a sophisticated scanner is activated and a blue light comes out of the door scanning Keno's entire body.

Computer Voice - You are not authorized to enter.

Keno - Say what!?

-Suddenly from the doors to the computer lab Keno's teenage friend Jimmy emerges.

Jimmy - Hey Keno. Sorry you couldn't get in. You need special clearance to enter.

Keno - Jimmy, what's up with the new advanced security system our school has?

Jimmy - Well the school didn't put it there. The FBI did since they're protecting my newest project.

Keno - Hold on. Why in the world is the FBI protecting one of your new special science projects?

Jimmy - Keno my long-time friend, I believe you know my special science projects are a bit too advanced for their own good. Because of that, the FBI is afraid some international terrorists might break into the school and use my projects for some evil scheme.

Keno - Jimmy, I don't know whether to be amazed or scared by you.

-The two teenage guys begin walking down the hallway.

Jimmy - So you must've come by to talk to me. What's going on?

Keno - Oh I guess I was just looking for any friend to talk to. I'm really bumming today.

Jimmy - Oh no. I've seen these facial expressions from you before. You were rejected by yet another girl you were crazy about? Am I correct?

Keno - Unfortunately yes. I mean my life really feels like it stinks sometimes. Unlike you I have no specific career path ahead of me right now, no clue on who the future Mrs. Keno is supposed to be, and...

Jimmy - ...you do have food, shelter, education, and... Hey. I thought you had that regular babysitting job taking care of that little girl in your neighborhood. That's a career sort of.

Keno - That's not a career. That's a – I'm a good friend of the family next door job. I mean I actually really do like taking care of that little girl Kaylyn but I'm not gonna make babysitting or nanny duties my full time career. The problem is I don't know what my future full time career should be.

Jimmy - Well man, I learned awhile back that when things feel like they're out of your control, you gotta step back and remember God does have it all together. He knows what's coming your way.

Keno - That's swell and all but I need something more concrete to help me right now.

Jimmy - Well that's not something to hold your breath on. But I'll be praying for you.

-Jimmy then rushes onwards as Keno leans against a locker still looking upset.

Keno - Hmm. Maybe I should...

-Suddenly a huge green light appears in front of Keno causing Keno to cover his eyes for several seconds. When Keno opens his eyes he sees a teenage girl slightly shorter than him but with similar skin and hair color to himself. Her name is Lauren.

Keno - Okay. Who are you exactly supposed to be girl?

Lauren - Wow dad, you sure do act different younger.

Keno - You just called me dad.

Lauren - I know. By the way, my name is Lauren and I'm your time traveling daughter from the future.

Keno - A time traveling daughter from the future. I really need some rest.

-Keno then immediately faints onto the floor.

Scene 2

-Keno opens his eyes just slightly seeing a figure near him.

Keno - Mom. Mom is that you?

Lauren - There, there now. You just collapsed really suddenly there.

Keno - Oh mom. I had this dream where some girl appeared saying she was my time traveling daughter from the future.

Lauren - Well I am your time traveling daughter from the future.

-Keno then immediately sits up straight and can see everything clearly again.

Keno - The future!

-Keno then takes a good look at Lauren who is sitting next to him in the hallway.

Keno - But... if you're from the future then that means you could be altering your past and I may now be changing my present or maybe it's your future or... Aw man. I hate the concept of time travel.

Lauren - Calm down dad. Let me help you up.

-Lauren helps Keno up as Keno can only look at Lauren with amazement now.

Keno - Wait a sec. You're my daughter?

Lauren - Yeah. We do have the same skin, hair, and eye color.

Keno - Yeah but... I just can't believe you on only that.

Lauren - Your friend Jimmy probably has technology that can validate my claim.

Keno - He does?

Scene 3

-In the living room of Keno's house, Keno is sitting in a chair watching Jimmy look at his lap top which is hooked up to wires that are wrapped around Lauren.

Keno - Wow Jimmy. You're the only guy I know that carries DNA scanning equipment in their back pack on any given day.

Jimmy - Hmm. Well there's no doubt about it Keno. Her DNA strands match up perfectly with yours. She's your daughter.

Lauren - Just like I said.

Keno - But what are you doing here exactly?

Lauren - That's the weird part. Future Jimmy was working on yet another crazy experiment that I was helping him with. I knew it had something to do with time travel and it was dangerous. Then there was some small explosion that we didn't expect to happen and I wound up here.

Jimmy - I'm gonna develop time travel one day? Sweet. I gotta start looking into that field of research right now. You have fun with your daughter Keno.

-Jimmy then rushes out of the house as Keno and Lauren are left sitting in the room.

Lauren - So dad... what do you wanna do?

Keno - I don't know. I guess talk.

Scene 4

-In the living room Keno and Lauren sit in front of the T.V. as Keno flips channels using the remote.

Lauren - Wow. A lot of these shows you're flipping by I usually see on the classic T.V. show network.

Keno - Okay, this is weird. I mean you're my daughter from the future. We should be having long interesting discussions with each other but I'm just here flipping channels.

Lauren - It's because you're nervous about future events happening that you won't be able to avoid.

Keno - Pretty much yeah.

-Suddenly the two hear a door bell ring.

Keno - Oh yeah. That's my little neighbor Kaylyn. She always comes by here every afternoon after school. I watch after her. Come on in Kaylyn! It's unlocked.

-The young girl Kaylyn runs into the house.

Kaylyn - Keno!

-Keno then puts his knees on the floor with a look of complete happiness on his face.

Keno - Kaylyn!

-The two give each other a big long hug then finally let go of the other.

Kaylyn - I finished my homework.

Keno - Great. Well I missed you during the school day.

Kaylyn - I missed you more.

Keno - Hmm. Well from that hug maybe you have me beat today. Anyway, why don't you get yourself a snack in the kitchen?

Kaylyn - Okay.

-Kaylyn gives Keno another quick strong hug and then rushes off into the kitchen. A smiling Lauren has watched everything that has just happened.

Lauren - You really care about her a lot don't you?

Keno - Yeah. She's awesome.

Lauren - Well let me tell you one thing about the future. You helped Aunt Kaylyn turn out to be someone really amazing.

Keno - Aunt Kaylyn?

Lauren - Well... Kaylyn really followed your example well when she helped babysit me. She was like a second mom to me.

Keno - So... speaking of moms... who exactly did I...

Lauren - Let's just say you eventually find the right woman. And you and mom became one of the strongest and most loving couples ever in my opinion.

Keno - Wow. It's good to know that part of my life works out.

Lauren - Hey. I've got an idea of what we can do. It's something you do a lot from my perspective. Whenever there's anything worth really celebrating you take the whole family out for ice cream.

Keno - You know I was sort of having a craving for ice cream.

-Kaylyn then rushes back into the room.

Kaylyn - All I heard were the words – ice cream. Let's go!

Scene 5

-In the high school hallway Jimmy is walking by himself and also talking to himself.

Jimmy - Hmm. I wonder if Lauren's temporal jump is either a paradox event or an alternate universe creation event. Both would be so awesome though.

-Jimmy's talking stops when he sees Lauren trying to open the door to the special laboratory.

Jimmy - What are you doing?

-Lauren nervously turns around but then gets calm.

Lauren - Oh well since I've seen your future laboratory I wanted to check out your present one. But I can see you've got a special security system here.

Jimmy - Yeah. Only me and a few other guys and teachers around school can get in. I was going to reprogram the computer to let Keno get in though.

Lauren - Well from the looks of it, even security systems in this decade work great. Anyway, I should go.

-Lauren quickly runs off leaving Jimmy standing slightly confused.

Scene 6

-In her bedroom, Kaylyn is being tucked into bed by Keno.

Kaylyn - So when are mom and dad gonna get home?

Keno - After you fall asleep if that's possible. Good night Kaylyn.

Kaylyn - Wait Keno.

-Kaylyn jumps out of bed and gives Keno a strong hug.

Kaylyn - I love you Keno.

Keno - I love you too Kaylyn. Now go to sleep.

-Kaylyn finally lets go of Keno and falls into her own bed. Keno leaves Kaylyn's room to see Lauren waiting for him outside in the bedroom hallway.

Lauren - You really do care about her.

Keno - Don't I care about her in the future?

Lauren - More than anything. You always said the three most important girls in your life are mom, me, and her. I mean Kaylyn would go on to think of you as her second dad. I mean who wouldn't want to think of you as someone like that. I mean you wind up being the coolest dad for me.

-A few tears begin to go down Keno's face.

Keno - I'm really glad to hear that.

Scene 7

-In the school hallway Keno is walking with a big smile on his face and great confidence in his walk. Jimmy then runs over to Keno.

Keno - Hey Jimmy. Man it's a beautiful day today.

Jimmy - Hey Keno. You seem to be in a good mood. What's going on? A girl finally decided to go out with you?

Keno - No but I know it will happen one day now. I've just been talking with Lauren. She has really put me in a good mood and has given me great hope for the future.

Jimmy - Oh yeah. By the way Keno, the other day Lauren was sort of wandering around the laboratory in a suspicious way and...

Keno - Hey. She probably knows more about that place that you do. Let her do whatever. Okay?

-Jimmy has a reluctant expression on his face.

Jimmy - Okay. Whatever you say Keno.

Scene 8

-Jimmy is walking down the hallway by himself again thinking out loud.

Jimmy - I wonder why I'm getting so suspicious about Lauren? Guess my mind still goes a little crazy when it comes to time travel.

Lauren's Voice - I have it.

-Jimmy stops. Then he carefully peaks around the corner to see Lauren holding a small portable device near the doorway to the laboratory. While using it Lauren is talking into a cell phone head set.

Lauren - I've just input the virus through the security system door. Within hours the system will be hack-able and you will have all the technology of this laboratory for yourselves.

Jimmy - Aw man. I've gotta tell Keno.

Scene 9

-In the living room of his house, Keno is putting on a jacket as Lauren walks in through the front door.

Lauren - Ready for our little jog?

Keno - I don't know. Think you'll be able to catch up with your old man?

Lauren - You're not old yet dad.

-From the front door Jimmy walks in looking slightly nervous.

Jimmy - Keno, hey. Can I talk to you... alone?

Keno - Sure man. Lauren, I'll meet you outside.

Lauren - Okay dad.

-Lauren rushes outside leaving just Keno and Jimmy in the room now.

Keno - So Jimmy, what's up?

Jimmy - It's Lauren... She's not your daughter.

-Keno's face immediately changes to a hostile one.

Keno - What!?

Jimmy - An hour ago I saw her messing with the laboratory door. She was talking into a head set about sending a virus into my computer system.

Keno - And did you check for viruses?

Jimmy - And do you know how long it takes to virus check a system as huge as mine? Look, I told you there could be people after my technology so...

Keno - No. Lauren is my daughter. She would never do such a thing. A daughter of mine never would.

Jimmy - Then maybe she isn't your daughter.

Keno - Then how do you explain her DNA matching up perfectly with mine?

Jimmy - I...I don't know. All I know is that she can't be trusted. I mean would a real time traveler really give out as much detail on the future as she has.

Keno - She looks up to me. I was the one that raised her and I don't want you saying lies about her.

Jimmy - You're only saying these things based on what only Lauren told you. Listen, if you can't trust one of your best friends then who can you trust?

Keno - I guess that would be a good question to think about.

-With an angry look on his face, Keno leaves the house.

Jimmy - Man. I know something isn't right about Lauren but why isn't this all adding up?

Scene 10

-Jimmy is scrolling through several pages of information on his lap top while sitting on a park bench. While working Jimmy is thinking out loud to himself.

Jimmy - Something isn't adding up. The scientific evidence I uncovered says that she has to be Keno's daughter. The DNA strands line up perfectly. She practically has the same DNA as Keno. Almost too much the same. Hey, that's it. Lauren's DNA is way too similar to Keno's. Aside from a few small alterations such as the fact she's a girl, her DNA is exactly the same as Keno. There's no other DNA mixed in here. Everybody has some DNA from both parents but Lauren only has one. It seems that someone was trying really hard to make Lauren so much like Keno that they made her too much like Keno. Now we've got real proof to work with.

Scene 11

-Keno and Lauren walk down the school hallway laughing.

Lauren - Geez. I didn't know you started getting slow in your teenage years.

Keno - Hey. Cut me some slack. So anyway, why do you want to check out Jimmy's lab?

Lauren - Oh, just because.

Keno - Well lucky for you he's now allowed me to access it.

Lauren - Good. Now I'll be able to grab exactly what I need.

-Keno stands in front of the laboratory door and it opens. Keno and Lauren enter the lab but suddenly find themselves surrounded by Jimmy and a dozen FBI agents.

Lead FBI Agent - Freeze. FBI. You young lady are in our custody now. Back away from that girl young man.

Keno - What's going on here?

Lead FBI Agent - That girl is not your future daughter.

Keno - Jimmy. Don't tell me you dragged the entire FBI into this.

Jimmy - It's true Keno. Her DNA isn't exactly perfect. It only matches you and no else. What she is: is a female clone of you. That's why she could pass off as your daughter so easily.

Lead FBI Agent - An enemy country has been trying to steal the technology of this laboratory but wanted to do it unnoticed. They believed they could enter by closely befriending one of Jimmy's friends; and what better person to get close to that friend, then a daughter.

Keno - No. That can't be true. Lauren, tell them it's not true.

-Lauren suddenly makes an evil style smirk.

Lauren - It is.

-Lauren immediately kicks Keno hard in the chest sending him falling to the ground. The FBI agents begin to move towards Lauren.

Lauren - Oh, please back up. Don't think I don't have a portable explosive device on me.

-Keno slowly gets up while looking at Lauren.

Keno - How did... why did...

Lauren - Like they said, an enemy country wanted the technology in here. So I was manufactured as a clone in a laboratory to simply get close to you. Close enough to get the technology here.

-Jimmy then holds out a small vile containing a green substance.

Jimmy - But you're no perfectly created human being. Every molecule in your body is unstable. I saw that after I studied my scans better. One drop of this chemical and you're done for.

-Moving fast Lauren immediately kicks the vile out of Jimmy's hand and catches it.

Lauren - Thanks for letting me know how to protect myself even better.

-Suddenly Keno tries pushing against Lauren with his fists trying to grab the green vile. Lauren pushes back and soon the two are pushing their own fists against each other.

Keno - How could you deceive me the way you did? You gave me so much motivation, so much hope for my future... and all from a lie! You gave me the perfect daughter and future I wish I could have one day... and now it's all gone!

-With one strong push Keno grabs the green vile and immediately has the chemical from it dump onto Lauren. Lauren's body suddenly begins to disappear as a look of pain immediately goes into her face.

Lauren - Aaaaahhhh!

Scene 12

-In his living room, Keno sits alone with his hand on his forehead and a very sad expression on his face. From nearby Jimmy sits down next to Keno.

Jimmy - How are you doing?

Keno - I could say fine... but that would be a lie. Just like what Lauren was.

Jimmy - Don't feel too bad about being played. She had us all fooled for a while.

Keno - Listen Jimmy, I'm sorry that I...

Jimmy - It's cool. We'll both make sure it won't happen again.

Keno - No. Not everything is cool. I was so convinced Lauren was my daughter. She said exactly what I wish would happen to me in the future. To learn that I become a good parent and role model. To know I found the right woman to marry that I would have a daughter with. To see that everything hard I do now would result in something good in the end. It was hard for me to destroy her... but it was even harder for me to deal with the fact that a good future still isn't guaranteed for me. I guess I'm right back where this all started.

Jimmy - You know what Keno; you are right back where you started. However that's not necessarily a bad thing. We may not have some time traveler around that knows the future... but we do have a God who knows what lies in our future and is always getting us ready for it. Remember, the good book says that He has plans to prosper you and not to harm you; plans to give you hope... and a future. I mean, even though our futures are unknown; Gods' love and power is not. Besides, he's the one that put us all on the Earth in the first place... and I know he wouldn't have created us unless he had a few good things planned for our futures.

-Keno and Jimmy both sit silent for a moment.

Keno - Thank you for reminding me that Jimmy.

Jimmy - No problem. I'll see you around.

-Jimmy leaves the house leaving Keno by himself again. Keno continues to sit looking upset. Suddenly Kaylyn quickly runs through the front door and gives Keno a big hug.

Kaylyn - Keno!

-Keno hugs Kaylyn trying to perk himself up a bit.

Keno - Hey Kaylyn, how was your day?

Kaylyn - Well I did really good on the quiz today. Thanks for helping me study.

Keno - Hey, you know I'm always here for you Kaylyn.

Kaylyn - You know Keno, you're kind of like my dad sometimes. I mean not like my real dad, it's just kind of like you're a second dad to me. You're gonna be a cool real dad to somebody one day.

-Kaylyn immediately hugs Keno again leaving Keno looking both surprised and happy. Keno begins to hug Kaylyn back as tears begin to appear in his eyes.

Keno - That's great to know.

THE END

Chapter 3 – A Valentine's Day Carol

Scene 1

-In a high school hallway a teenage girl: Kaitlyn is banging her head against a locker. As she bangs her head against the locker, her male friend: Jimmy walks over to her with a concerned and confused look on his face.

Jimmy - Uh… Kaitlyn… why are you banging your head against your locker?

Kaitlyn - It's February 14th and I'm clutching in my hand an opened valentine that I created for somebody else. Figure it out!

Jimmy - Well I think it would help me a lot if I didn't have to deal with the sound of you banging your head against your locker.

-Kaitlyn stops banging her head against her locker so she can look right at Jimmy. Her face is that of an annoyed and sad person.

Kaitlyn - I spent hours creating the perfect Valentine's Day card for the always so handsome Bill Paxton, as a way for me to share my undying feelings of love with him. But then I show him my card and he tells me he got a girlfriend two days ago. Two days Jimmy!

Jimmy - Kaitlyn, this is like a broken record deal with you. I mean I've known you for years and this has always been the case with you. You try to tell some handsome guy you like how you feel about him, and he rejects you.

Kaitlyn - Yes. It's a never-ending cycle for me. Jimmy, I'm in high school now and I still have never been in a stable boyfriend/girlfriend relationship.

Jimmy - Hey, I'm in high school and I haven't either.

Kaitlyn - That's different Jimmy. You're a nerd.

Jimmy - And what is that supposed to mean?

Kaitlyn - Nothing. Look. Heartbreak is the only consistency I have in my life. Do you know what it's like to have your heart suffer?

Jimmy - Well there was that lab rat the psychology class kept having run through mazes. My heart just couldn't stand to see a living creature treated like some sort of slave. So I gave the lab rat a miniature exo-suit with plasma cannons so it could escape from its' confinement. Of course those plasma cannons also destroyed an entire wing of the school building.

Kaitlyn - You're getting off topic. Look, I believe I deserve some happy romance in my life. Yet I'm not getting it. I'm ready for one though. So what's the deal!?

Jimmy - Well if you want me to get a bit deep, I have learned recently that sometimes the good Lord's timing doesn't always match with our own. But we do need to remember that he's got a plan better than anything we could come up with.

Kaitlyn - A better plan!? So far the plan has only left me in heartbreak! I'm telling you Jimmy. Love is dead, and Valentine's Day has gone down with it. Bah hum bug!

Scene 2

-It is night time at her house, and Kaitlyn is walking up the stairs towards her bedroom.

Kaitlyn - Man all of those lovey dovey movies on TV are so fake. Man, I need some sleep.

-As Kaitlyn climbs up the stairs she begins to hear the sounds of chains.

Kaitlyn - Hold on. Are those chains I hear?

-As Kaitlyn continues to climb up the stairs, the sound of chains gets louder.

Kaitlyn - Okay, this is getting scary. I just want to get in bed now.

-Kaitlyn dashes into her room, locks the door, grabs a baseball bat, and then jumps into her bed looking scared. Suddenly she begins to hear an eerie voice making grunt noises.

Kaitlyn - Who's out there!?

-Suddenly through the door a ghost in the form of a preschool girl appears floating above the ground.

Kaitlyn - Ahh! You're a ghost and you look just like my best friend from Pre-K: Kelly. But hold on... if you're a ghost and you look just like Kelly, then does that mean...

Kelly - No, no, no. I am just the ghost of your memory of your Pre-K friend: Kelly. I am here to warn you Kaitlyn.

Kaitlyn - Warn me about what? This isn't Halloween.

Kelly - Just shut your mouth girl so I can talk! Tonight you shall be visited by three spirits that represent different points in time. Listen closely to the message they bring you Kaitlyn... or else!

Kaitlyn - Or else what?

Kelly - Or else... Uh... I didn't really think that part through. But beware Kaitlyn! Beware!

-The Kelly ghost then goes through the door and disappears.

Kaitlyn - Wow. I was just visited by a ghost who told me three more ghosts are gonna visit me later. I should so make that my Facebook status right now. But I really should go to sleep.

-Kaitlyn then lays down and begins to fall asleep.

Scene 3

-A few hours later Kaitlyn is asleep in her bed. Suddenly Kaitlyn begins to wake up as she can sense the presence of a spirit entering her room. Kaitlyn opens her eyes and sees a male ghost hovering over her with an afro, bell bottoms, and a mood ring. Kaitlyn immediately jumps out of bed.

Kaitlyn - Ahh! Who the heck are you!

Ghost - Chill your vibes little missy. I am the Ghost of Valentine's Day Past. But you can call me – "Old School", because when you're a ghost that represents the past, you've got to kick it old school.

Kaitlyn - Okay... So what are you here to do with me?

Old School Ghost - I'm here to force you to look at your past.

Kaitlyn - So what are you gonna do? Snap your fingers and have us appear in my childhood?

Old School Ghost - You think I have time travel technology? I'm the ghost of Valentine's Day past? I still have one of those large clunky cell phones that went out with the 80's. We're gonna look back at your past using ancient technology.

-Old School Ghost then pulls out a TV with an attached VCR, and then inserts a VHS tape. Old School Ghost then pulls out a couch and Kaitlyn sits in it.

Old School Ghost - Now sit back and relax girl. By the way you want some nice tasting high in fat popcorn? It's from the days before low-fat was in.

-The two then see on the TV screen a Pre-K age Kaitlyn is playing blocks with her friend Kelly.

Pre-K Kelly - I'm gonna have a boyfriend before any other girl in this class does.

Pre-K Kaitlyn - Na-uh. I'll get a boyfriend first.

-Pre-K Kaitlyn then grabs a pink paper heart and goes over to a Pre-K boy.

Pre-K Kaitlyn - Hi Bobby. I made you a Valentine's Day card. Do you wanna be my boyfriend?

Bobby - No way. Girls have cooties.

-Bobby then walks away leaving Pre-K Kaitlyn with a sad look on her face. Meanwhile present day Kaitlyn also has a sad face.

Kaitlyn - That was my first childhood heartbreak. Ever since then I've been searching relentlessly to find the one true love of my life.

Old School Ghost - And because you couldn't find the true love you sought out, you assumed love must not be real.

Kaitlyn - I've seen too much! Get out of here ghost. I want to get rid of you! Who do I call to get rid of a ghost like you?

Old School Ghost - Who you gonna call? Ghostbusters!

Kaitlyn - What?

Old School Ghost - Sorry. I'm old school, remember. Don't worry though. I'm gone.

-Old School Ghost then floats through the door and disappears. Kaitlyn then jumps back into her bed trying to fall asleep again.

Scene 4

-Kaitlyn while lying in her bed opens her eyes.

Kaitlyn - Man. Falling back asleep is harder than it looks.

-Kaitlyn then notices a wrapped present on the ground of her room in the shape of a heart. Kaitlyn walks over to the present.

Kaitlyn - Where'd this present come from? Hmm, it smells like a fruit cake.

-Kaitlyn opens up the present and from it a ghost in the form of a modern day teenage girl pops out.

Ghost - Who are you calling a fruitcake sister!?

Kaitlyn - Ahh! Who are you?

-The ghost then points to the present she just popped out of.

Ghost - I'm the Ghost of Valentine's Day Present. It's a pun, get it? But you can call me *Present*.

Kaitlyn - So what have you come to do with me?

Present Ghost - I'm here to show you your present, duh.

Kaitlyn - Hey. Are you gonna grab my hand and have us fly out of here and go over to somebody else's house and see what they're doing through the window.

Present Ghost - Fly to somebody else's house? Who do you think I am? Mary Poppins? Hold on.

-Present Ghost then gets out her cell phone and begins texting a message into it as she says out loud was she's texting.

Present Ghost - OMG. This new job is so not - LOL.

Kaitlyn - So what are we gonna do?

-Present Ghost then jumps in front of a computer.

Present Ghost - We're gonna use one of the small surveillance devices the government inserts in everybody's home to see how a friend of yours is doing.

Kaitlyn - Hold on. What did you just say about the government and surveillance devices?

Present Ghost - Hold on. There, I got it. A current feed of your friend Jimmy's house.

-Kaitlyn looked at the computer screen to see Jimmy in his bedroom with a card in his hand.

Kaitlyn - Why's Jimmy staring blankly at that card?

Present Ghost - Just be quiet and watch.

-On the screen Jimmy is seen opening up the card revealing that it's shows a collage of pictures of him and Kaitlyn together at various ages in their life.

Jimmy - Every year I try to find the nerve to give Kaitlyn a Valentine's Day card. And the year I finally feel ready to do so, she decides love is dead along with Valentine's Day. I wish I could figure out a way to make her realize that isn't true. Oh well. I guess me and her aren't meant to be.

-Kaitlyn's face becomes very surprised.

Kaitlyn - I... I had no idea that Jimmy felt...

Present Ghost - Yeah, well he did. And just wait until the third ghost shows you what your actions in the present have done to your future.

Kaitlyn - I... I think I'm a little too afraid to meet this third ghost now.

Present Ghost - Well... I'm sorry... but he's coming whether you like it or not.

-Present Ghost then floats out of the room and disappears. Kaitlyn is left standing with a scared and uncertain look on her face.

Scene 5

-Kaitlyn sits on her bed looking terrified.

Kaitlyn - Okay. I'm not gonna be afraid of this third ghost. I'm not gonna be afraid.

-Suddenly a gust of wind comes into Kaitlyn's room. Slowly emerging from the door appears a ghost wearing a very dark cloak and hood. The silent ghost slowly walks over to Kaitlyn's bed as Kaitlyn can only sit in a nervous position.

-Kaitlyn - Are you... are you the... are you the Ghost of Valentine's Day Future?

-Suddenly the ghost takes off his dark hood to show he has pointed hears and is wearing a red fez on his head.

Ghost - Yes I am human lady. My name is "Future", and I wish for you to live long and prosper.

Kaitlyn - Hold on. Why does a ghost representing the future look like an alien?

Future Ghost - Because I represent a future in which aliens and humans live on Earth together in peace. Although there was that huge war that the humans provoked leading to a huge...

Kaitlyn - Hold on. I have an even more important question. What in the name of sanity is on your head!?

Future Ghost - Oh, it's a fez. I wear a fez now. Fezzes are cool.

Kaitlyn - Whatever. Now then... what are you here for?

Future Ghost - To show you your future.

-Future Ghost then gets out a small communicator device and speaks into it.

Future Ghost - Scotty, beam us to the future!

-Then in a flash of glittering light, Future Ghost and Kaitlyn disappear.

Scene 6

-On an outdoor sidewalk at night, no one is present. Then in a brilliant burst of light, Future Ghost and Kaitlyn appear.

Kaitlyn - So where are we?

Future Ghost - The future young padawan. What did you expect?

Kaitlyn - So... what do you want me to see?

Future Ghost - Just look over there.

-Kaitlyn turns her head to the left and sees a huge grave yard.

Kaitlyn - The cemetery!? No!!!!

Future Ghost - Whoa. Calm down girl. Not over there. Over there. To your right.

-Kaitlyn turns her head again and this time sees a retirement home.

Kaitlyn - Oh. A retirement home.

Future Ghost - Look. Let's just look in that window over there. There's something I want to show you.

-Kaitlyn and Future Ghost go over to the window to see a very old looking Kaitlyn sitting in a chair watching TV.

Kaitlyn - Whoa! Is that me!?

Future Ghost - Yep. About eighty years from now. Do you see anything strange with this picture?

Kaitlyn - Yeah. The future me is watching Star Wars on the TV when we all know that show starring a certain time traveler in a blue box is so much better.

Future Ghost - Stop looking at the TV. Look. You're living all alone and there are no pictures anywhere here indicating a past relationship of any kind.

-The two then see inside the retirement home, an elderly man walking into the room.

Elderly Man - Well hi Kaitlyn. It's Valentine's Day and since we are the only single people on our floor, maybe we should go to dinner together.

Old Kaitlyn - No way. Love doesn't exist and neither should Valentine's Day.

Elderly Man - Kaitlyn, I know I'm not the first man in this retirement home you've rejected. I don't know what terrible heartbreak you experienced long ago that caused you to become what you are today, but you can't let your sad past keep you from experiencing a wonderful present or future.

Old Kaitlyn - Like any of that is really true. Just leave me alone. Bah hum bug.

-The elderly man walks away as present day Kaitlyn steps back looking shocked.

Kaitlyn - I can't believe it. By acting like love is dead, I blinded myself from every potential romance in my future that could've worked out. I end up becoming worse than all of the people that rejected me.

Future Ghost - Yes. You're correct.

Kaitlyn - I can't take this anymore. I want another chance. Please! I want another chance!!!

Scene 7

-Kaitlyn suddenly jumps out of her bed realizing she is in her bedroom.

Kaitlyn - Hey. I'm in my bedroom. Was that all a dream?

-Kaitlyn then runs over to her bedroom window and opens it up. Outside Kaitlyn sees a little boy walking down the street.

Kaitlyn - You there! What day is it?

Little Boy - It's the day after Valentine's Day ma'am.

Kaitlyn - Okay, it's just the day after. There's still hope.

-Kaitlyn then gets out her purse as she looks at the boy.

Kaitlyn - Hey kid. Can I hand you some money so you can buy some Valentine's Day card for me?

Little Boy - No way! I don't accept money from strangers.

Kaitlyn - Good lifestyle choice to live by. I guess I'll have to start working fast.

Scene 8

-Jimmy walks down the sidewalk towards the high school with an upset look on his face. Suddenly Kaitlyn from far away begins running towards Jimmy.

Kaitlyn - Jimmy! Wait up!

-Jimmy turns to look at Kaitlyn.

Jimmy - Kaitlyn?

-Kaitlyn soon catches up with Jimmy and holds out a small picture frame.

Kaitlyn - I wanted to give you this.

-Jimmy accepts the picture frame and sees inside of it is a picture of him and Kaitlyn holding hands when they were much younger.

Jimmy - Whoa. This is from way back. We haven't held hands in years.

Kaitlyn - I found it in my room this morning and decided to frame it. Think of it as a late Valentine's Day gift from one friend to another.

Jimmy - Valentine's Day? I thought you didn't believe in that holiday?

Kaitlyn - Well a really bizarre experience got me thinking. I shouldn't let a couple of bad experiences in romance make me feel down, at least not for a long time. Especially since it might cause me to ignore a real romance that the good Lord might send my way one day.

-Jimmy's face begins to go slightly red as he begins to put the picture frame in his backpack. As he attempts to do he begins to accidentally lose his balance. Kaitlyn suddenly helps Jimmy by having her hand grab onto Jimmy's.

Kaitlyn - I've got you. Now let's get going. Don't want to miss what's coming up next today.

-Kaitlyn and Jimmy then both continue walking to school together without making any comment related to their hands still holding on to one another.

THE END

Chapter 4 – The Sick Day

Scene 1

-In a high school hallway - a teenage girl: Kaitlyn is talking to somebody on her cell phone. She is in the middle of a conversation.

Kaitlyn - He still has a fever? And it's not looking any better? It may be getting worse? Well thank you ma'am. Tell Jimmy that I hope he gets better.

Kaitlyn then puts away her phone as her female friend Monica walks up to her.

Monica - Hey Kaitlyn. How ya doin?

Kaitlyn - I'm fine but Jimmy isn't. I called his house and his mom said that Jimmy's fever is only getting worse.

Monica - That sounds awful. Is someone staying home with him?

Kaitlyn - Well his mom has to leave their house soon, which will leave Jimmy alone for about five hours.

Monica - That's too bad. It's already tough enough that he's missing mid-term exams right now. Well hopefully he'll get better by the exam make up day. Anyway, I gotta get to class.

-Monica then begins to walk away causing Kaitlyn to think hard for a moment.

Kaitlyn - Wait a minute. The exam make up day. That's it.

Scene 2

-In a small living room, Jimmy is laying down on a couch. He has a pillow behind his head and a blanket covering most of his body. Jimmy looks up at the ceiling as has a very sick look on his face.

Jimmy - Well... mom is gone now. And here I am. Laying here all alone, feeling so sick and exhausted. What is someone like me in this condition supposed to do?

-Jimmy's spoken thoughts are suddenly interrupted by Kaitlyn walking into the living room with a plate and glass of water.

Kaitlyn - What you're going to do and stay on the couch as I give you this medicine along with this glass of water.

-Jimmy looks at Kaitlyn with a very surprised look on his face.

Jimmy - Kaitlyn!? What are you doing here?

Kaitlyn - I called earlier and your mom told me that you were gonna be here alone for five hours. Soon after that, I told her that I would love to help take care of you during that time. She seemed cool with it, and so now here I am.

Jimmy - But... what about your exams?

Kaitlyn - I'll just take them during the makeup day. Which you will as well.

Jimmy - But I'm not getting any better right now. In fact, I may never be in school again if this fever of mine keeps getting worse.

Kaitlyn - Believe me Jimmy. You will be better by the time the makeup day comes.

Jimmy - And what makes you so sure of yourself?

-Kaitlyn then holds the glass of water she was holding closer to Jimmy's face.

Kaitlyn - Because I've got water and medicine here. Now drink up!

Jimmy - But I'm still feeling...

Kaitlyn - Now!

-Jimmy quickly swallows the medicine and water that Kaitlyn has given him.

Jimmy - Gee. You didn't have to shove it down my throat.

-Kaitlyn then holds a plate with toast on it closer to Jimmy's face.

Kaitlyn - I've got toast. It's buttery. Now eat it!

-Jimmy then quickly eats the toast. As Jimmy swallows the last of his food, Kaitlyn sits in a chair next to Jimmy. Jimmy then clears his throat and looks right at Kaitlyn.

Jimmy - Kaitlyn. What is up with you right now!? You're shouting demands at me to eat food and drink water.

Kaitlyn - Is it wrong to ask a friend to do something to make his life better?

Jimmy - Well... no.

Kaitlyn - Jimmy, there are so many people in this world who know how to live a healthy and good lifestyle. Yet they shut their mouths so often and continue to allow other people around them to live their lives however they feel like. Well I'm not gonna be like that.

Jimmy - Wow. That's pretty deep.

Kaitlyn - Thank you.

Jimmy - So... wanna check out what cartoons are on cable right now?

Kaitlyn - Sounds cool.

Scene 3

-Jimmy and Kaitlyn are both watching a television program that's on in the living room.

Kaitlyn - The character in the show just said – telescopular. What does that word mean?

Jimmy - It means... uh... just give me my dictionary and I'll tell you.

-Kaitlyn gets up and then begins walking towards a computer.

Kaitlyn - Or I could just look it up online really quick. It's faster with the internet.

Jimmy - Kaitlyn. Looking up a definition in a book is much faster than the internet.

Kaitlyn - But with a book you have to flip through so many pages. It takes too long.

Jimmy - Yes but when any teenager goes to look up something on the internet, first they must check their e-mail, Facebook, Twitter, and YouTube accounts before doing anything else. That takes much longer. Thus, using books is still faster.

Kaitlyn - Ouch. Okay then. One point for you.

-Jimmy then raises one arm in the air with pride.

Jimmy - Yeah!

-Then suddenly Jimmy feels a sharp pain going through his body and begins to moan in pain. Kaitlyn quickly moves closer to Jimmy with a look of concern on her face.

Kaitlyn - Jimmy. Are you okay? You really don't look well.

Jimmy - Um, I'm fine Kaitlyn. I guess I just pulled a muscle.

-Kaitlyn then puts her right hand on Jimmy's forehead.

Kaitlyn - Your head is getting really hot. We have to get you better soon of you'll end up in the hospital.

Jimmy - Look Kaitlyn. You've given me all of the types of medicine I can take. Let's just wait around and see if the effects from those medications kick in soon.

Kaitlyn - Yeah well until then, I'm gonna make you some tea.

-Kaitlyn then stands up and begins to walk into the nearby kitchen.

Jimmy - Tea!? You're gonna make me tea? What's gonna be the point in that?

Kaitlyn - It's a special kind of tea my grandmother showed me how to make. You mix a tiny bit of these special herbs, a dash of coffee, and... well, just take my word for it. It'll work.

-As Kaitlyn prepares the tea in the kitchen Jimmy calls out to her.

Jimmy - Kaitlyn, you really don't have to be here. There's nothing good that can come from my being sick. You're just gonna wind up being miserable for the same amount of time as me now.

-Kaitlyn then walks back into the living room with a cup of tea in her hands.

Kaitlyn - Jimmy, do you really believe that only bad things can come out of undesirable events?

Jimmy - Well good days can still occur after bad days, but a bad day is still a bad day.

Kaitlyn - I'm not gonna deny the fact that a painful experience is always gonna be painful. But didn't you listen carefully to the sermon the pastor at church said a few weeks ago. There's that verse in the good book that says how the Lord causes all things to work together for good to those who love him. Not some things. All things.

-Jimmy is beginning to look a bit lost for words.

Jimmy - Yeah, but...

-Kaitlyn then has both of her hands touch Jimmy's hands.

Kaitlyn - Jimmy. I don't know why you've become sick. But trust me. Somewhere in the big scheme of things, God is using this to help work towards something amazing. And until that happens, I'll stay by your side Jimmy... because I... kinda... really like you... a lot.

-Suddenly Jimmy's face begins to look very red. Kaitlyn notices this and begins to look worried.

Kaitlyn - Jimmy. Your face is getting kinda red. Are you starting to feel more sick?

Jimmy - Uh, no. I'm just fine. In fact... I'm starting to feel better.

Scene 4

-Jimmy is still lying on the couch as Kaitlyn is beginning to put a backpack on her back.

Kaitlyn - Sorry I have to go now but someone has to look after my younger brother. Your mom did say she would be home in a few minutes.

Jimmy - She did. Thanks for spending the afternoon with me Kaitlyn. I... kinda enjoyed it.

-A big smile can be seen on Kaitlyn's face.

Kaitlyn - Awesome. Well I'll... see you later then.

-Kaitlyn then leaves the house through the front door and begins to walk away from it. Jimmy watches her through a window as she walks away. Once Kaitlyn is out of sight, Jimmy looks up.

Jimmy - Okay Lord. I think I understand a little better now how you really do cause all things to work together for good.

THE END

Chapter 5 – Painful Heartbreak

Scene 1

-In a long hallway with lots of fancy paintings and plants, three teenagers: Keno, Jimmy, and Kaitlyn are walking down together. Keno and Jimmy are both wearing black tuxedos while Kaitlyn is wearing a long light pink dress.

Kaitlyn – This is so awesome Jimmy! I can't believe I'm getting the chance to attend a real royal wedding.

Jimmy – Well after I was allowed to share some of my inventions and scientific knowledge with the king, he was so grateful that he wanted to invite me and any of my friends to come to his daughter's wedding.

Keno – And how come we've never heard of this king and his country before?

Jimmy – Because he's no traditional king. Just a billionaire who owns his very own personal island, got it declared as an independent country, and named himself king.

Keno – Ah, so we're not technically dealing with royalty. We're dealing with super rich folk.

Kaitlyn – I don't care. What it means is we'll be getting fancy food, ballroom dancing, and...

Jimmy – Getting the chance to meet a handsome prince?

Kaitlyn – Well I don't have to look forward to that. I'm already walking right next to one.

-Jimmy's face suddenly becomes red as he turns away from Kaitlyn to look at Keno.

Jimmy – So Keno, think you'll meet some nice people at the wedding?

Kaitlyn – Ooo. Like a beautiful princess? An amazing young lady whom upon first glance, you fall in love with?

Keno – What? You think I'm gonna fall for a girl that I just start interacting with at a wedding? That stuff doesn't happen to me.

-Kaitlyn rolls her eyes.

Kaitlyn – Sure. Whatever you say.

Scene 2

-In a large church like sanctuary, the wedding begins. Sitting in the middle amongst a hundred people are Keno, Jimmy, and Kaitlyn; all of whom are sitting close together.

Keno – Things sure are moving slowly.

Jimmy – What did you expect? Weddings are always so slow.

Kaitlyn – That way, everyone can take in every single detail of this most beautiful day… and I already feel like crying.

Keno – Kaitlyn, how can you get emotional about a wedding where you don't know anybody?

Kaitlyn – I don't care if I don't know anybody. I'm watching a version of what I've always fantasized my own future will one day look like. Isn't that right Jimmy?

Jimmy – Um, why does it matter that I agree with that statement?

-Kaitlyn's face suddenly turns red as she turns away from Jimmy.

Kaitlyn – Oh... no reason.

-Suddenly the three hear music playing on an organ.

Jimmy – Okay, let's be quiet. That music must mean that the bride will be coming down the aisle soon.

-Keno glances to his left and sees several people of various ages in fancy clothes slowly walking towards the front of the room. Keno turns away.

Keno – Eh. Already bored.

Kaitlyn – Hey look over there. That must be the flower girl. Hmm. A little older than a typical flower girl. She looks like she's around our age.

-Keno glances and sees a teenage girl walking down the aisle with flowers in her hand. Her eyes, hair, and dress all reflect sunlight from a nearby open window as Keno finds himself starring at her.

Keno – Whoa.

Jimmy – Hey Keno. Your face doesn't look well. You feeling all right?

Keno – I feel fine Jimmy. It's just... I'm experiencing some weird feelings inside myself. Um... Jimmy, do you know who that flower girl is?

Jimmy – Hmm. Oh yeah. I saw her briefly during my interactions with the king. That is Princess Ashley. The king's second and only other child.

Keno – Hmm. Princess Ashley...

Scene 3

-In a large dining hall, several people slowly walk in. Already sitting together at a table are Keno, Jimmy, and Kaitlyn.

Kaitlyn – So many weddings have kid's tables. I get it. But we're teenagers now. We should be allowed to sit with the adults. But nope. They continue to segregate us by making a teenager's table. It's an outrage I tell you. But what's an even bigger outrage is that we can't even eat yet.

Jimmy – Kaitlyn, we can't start eating until all of the other guests arrive, not to mention the bridge and groom. It's all about being polite.

Kaitlyn – I'll tell you what's not polite! Making a teenager starve near fancy wedding food. I want my wedding food fill and I want it now!

-As Kaitlyn and Jimmy continue to talk, Keno sits at the table constantly folding and unfolding a napkin in front of him with a slightly nervous expression in his face. Jimmy and Kaitlyn stop talking as they notice this.

Jimmy – Hey Keno. You look like something is on you mind.

Keno – Why isn't everyone here yet? It's been twenty minutes.

-Suddenly the teenage girl, Princess Ashley sits right next to Keno.

Ashley – I'll say. I would've come in here immediately. But I've got tons of uncles and aunts who just couldn't stop talking to me and saying how big I've gotten. Oh, by the way. My name's Princess Ashley.

Jimmy – Oh, hello there. My name is Jimmy and these are my friends.

Ashley – Yes, Jimmy. The teenage inventor whose work highly impressed my father. It's an honor to meet you.

Jimmy – Likewise. By the way, these are my friends Keno and Kaitlyn.

-Kaitlyn then moves Jimmy's chair far from Ashley's as she begins to talk.

Kaitlyn – Yes and the only female that Jimmy will be sitting next to tonight will be me, because of… reasons.

-Kaitlyn then scoots Keno's chair close to Ashley's.

Kaitlyn – But Keno is free to sit next to anyone. Enjoy yourselves.

-Kaitlyn then quickly sits down next to Jimmy. Both Keno and Ashley look at the other as the two smile slightly.

Keno – Yeah, I'm Keno. Jimmy invited me. Anyway… um… it was a nice wedding ceremony.

Ashley – Oh yes. My older sister Grace has been planning this wedding for months. She always knew her now husband was the one for her. She is serious when it comes to romance.

Keno – Wow. That sounds awesome.

Ashley – So tell me about yourself Keno. What are your hobbies?

Keno – Well amongst several things, I like to dabble in drawing and writing stories.

Ashley – Well I'm not big into drawing.

-Keno tilts his head down.

Keno – Oh.

Ashley – But I really do like writing stores.

-Keno tilts his head up.

Keno – Oh.

Ashley – Yeah. I mean I recently finished this one story that a lot of people I know seem to like.

Keno – Really? Well tell me about it.

Ashley – Well it's about these two families that are feuding. But then one day a man and a woman from the two different families meet and they fall in love.

Keno – Like in Romeo and Juliet.

Ashley – Yeah but in my story, despite the pressure put on them by their families, they run away from their homes and live happily ever after.

Keno – Hmm. Sounds like a very interesting story.

Scene 4

-About two hours later, Keno and Ashley are still sitting in the same positions near each other but are now both laughing.

Ashley – Amazing joke Keno. Amazing.

Keno – Thank you. I aim to please.

Ashley – Wow. It's been two hours and I can't believe how much fun we've had talking and getting to know one another. You know I never thought I'd have so much in common with... someone who's not royalty.

Keno – And I never thought I'd have so much in common with a princess.

Ashley – Well if you excuse me, we have been sitting for a while. I need to get up and move... and also use the bathroom.

Keno – Go right ahead.

-Ashley gets up and walks away. Seconds later Jimmy walks over and sits next to Keno.

Jimmy – Hey Keno. You and Ashley have been talking for quite a while. So what's getting to know a princess feel like?

Keno – Jimmy, she is the most perfect girl I have ever met. She's kind, funny, creative, and it seems like she really cares about other people.

Jimmy – Um, Keno. I know you went through a tough falling out with another girl recently, but I'm seeing that look in your eyes and I have to ask you... do you think what you're feeling and what you're thinking about doing next is right? I mean... she's a princess.

Keno – A perfect princess Jimmy. And to both questions... I believe the answer is... yes.

-Suddenly Kaitlyn zooms over and sits right next to Keno.

Kaitlyn – Oh, Keno. I know the past love of your life broke your heart, stomped it, and then destroyed it with a machine gun, but don't let that stop you from taking a chance with this princess who may mend your heart and make your life become something more.

Jimmy – Kaitlyn, where do you get dialogue like that from?

Kaitlyn – My therapist… maybe. I'm not really sure. Sometimes I question if our sessions together really are proving effective.

Scene 5

-About another two hours later, Keno and Ashley are sitting together again talking with one another.

Keno – So yeah, not only do I help take care of a couple of the young kids in my neighborhood, but I also just started volunteering at this cool after school care place and am helping take care of young kids there as well.

Ashley – That sounds awesome. You know I like to help take care of young kids as well. It's such an awesome experience

Keno – I know. Why don't other people realize this?

Ashley – Well to be honest Keno, you're the first teenage guy I've ever met who likes to work with little kids. I mean let me tell you, my boyfriend hates little kids.

Keno – Boyfriend?

Ashley – Ex-boyfriend.

Keno – Oh.

Ashley – He was just some rich guy I thought could understand me but he couldn't. Not only did we have not much in common, but he treated me different around his friends. He'd act like I was the only thing he cared about when it was just me and him. Then you threw just one of his friends into the picture and he'd act like I was some trash he carried around. So I just stayed away from him after that.

Keno – That's awful. You know I act the same around all of my friends. I don't put on an act for anybody. The only persona you should show people is the persona of you at your best. And that's what everyone needs to know.

Ashley – Wow Keno. You just make so much sense and you listen to and understand me so well.

Keno – Hey. You too.

Ashley – So Keno… do you have any sort of… girlfriend back home or anything?

Keno – Well… no. I'm not exactly a lucky in love kind of person. There was a friend of mine awhile back. Her name was Casey. We had been friends for so long and I became attracted to her for months, but when I finally told her how I felt… she turned me down.

Ashley – Oh, that sounds terrible. Awhile back I tried to make some handsome guy I knew like me. But when I eventually realized that he had no interest in me, at the time it left me feeling devastated… and sometimes I still feel that way.

Keno – I know. Even when you feel like you've gotten over it, somehow from time to time you still feel the pain from that heart breaking moment.

-Suddenly a wedding host holding a microphone appears near the two and begins to speak to everyone in the room.

Host – Hello everyone. Hope you've enjoyed this very long wedding lunch. But now it's time for the traditional wedding dance. The bride and groom shall come onto the dance floor, and any other happy couples may join them on the floor as well.

-Slow dance music begins to play. The bride and groom begin to slowly dance together and soon, other couples get on to the dance floor and begin to slowly dance as well. As the dancing continues, Keno and Ashley both begin to look up.

Keno – So... um... Ashley. Do you want to maybe... I don't know... do you want to...

Ashely – Dance with you?

Keno – Well... yeah.

Ashley – I'd love to.

-Keno and Ashley both get up and walk to the middle of the dance floor. Ashley puts her hands on Keno's shoulder and Keno holds Ashley's arms with his hands. The two begin to slowly dance together as both of them find themselves caught looking into the other's eyes. Ashley then moves her body closer to Keno's as she begins to close her eyes.

Ashley – Keno... this may be one of the most amazing moments of my life.

-Keno smiles as he holds Ashley close to him.

Keno – Mine too.

Scene 6

-Some time later Ashley is pulling Keno's hand as she leads him past several tables.

Ashley – Come on Keno. You have to meet my father: King Percy. I know he'll like you.

-Both Keno and Ashley reach a large table where a man and a woman both with robes and crowns on are sitting.

Ashley – Keno, these are my parents: King Percy and Queen Belle. Mom. Dad. This is Keno. One of the friends of the kind young inventor that you invited. He's very kind and sweet and as we've been hanging out for the last few hours we've realized that we have a lot in common. I really like him.

King Percy – Well that's nice.

Queen Belle – Why Ashley, have you spoken to you sister at all this afternoon? Come, let's both talk to her and ask her how it feels to finally be married.

Ashley – Oh, sure. I'll see you in a bit Keno.

-Ashley and Queen Belle both walk away leaving both Keno and King Percy alone.

King Percy – So Keno, you and my daughter seem to be very fond of each other.

Keno – Oh yeah. She is a really amazing person.

King Percy – You know I am very wealthy. Tell you what. Name anything you want and I'll buy it for you it. Gadgets, machines, even buildings. Name it and it's yours.

Keno – Really? That's so nice of you. But is there some catch? Do I have to do anything in return?

King Percy – Yes. You must stay away from my daughter!

Keno – What!?!

Scene 7

-Some time later, sitting together at a table are Keno, Jimmy, and Kaitlyn. Jimmy and Kaitlyn both have concerned looks on their faces as Keno talks to them.

Keno – And after he told me stay away from his daughter, I of course asked why. And then he said it's because I'm some simple commoner who could never be able to provide for his royal daughter.

Jimmy – That's awful.

Kaitlyn – Yeah, this really stinks. It's discrimination based on someone's financial status. I mean, it's something you have very little control over when you're young.

Keno – The biggest problem now though is what I am going to tell Ashley. I mean, we just met earlier today but I see so much potential in what a future with her could be like.

Jimmy – But that's the thing though Keno. You just met her today. What did you plan on gaining today with someone you've just met?

Keno – It's not about what I hope to gain anymore Jimmy! It's about what I might be losing! Ugg. I finally meet someone that actually does want to be with me, but her father is going to act as some big road block between us! Err!

Jimmy – Well... you have to do something now.

Keno – Yeah... and I'll start with telling Ashley the truth. The whole truth.

Scene 8

-Some time later, Keno and Ashley are both sitting together alone at a table.

Ashley – It was so funny when my sister got the wedding cake stuffed in her face. Everyone that saw it was howling. So Keno, you said you wanted to ask me something?

Keno – Yeah. Ashley... I know we've just met but based on what I've learned about you... I really like you... and I wanted to ask you if you really liked me.

Ashley – Well... we have just met but... yes, I do like you.

Keno – Well it's great to know that you like me... but your father doesn't.

Ashley – What do you mean?

Keno – Ashley, your father already guessed how we feel about each other and he doesn't want us to be together. He was trying to bribe me into staying away from you.

Ashley – HE WHAT!?!

Scene 9

-Moments later Ashley is running through the room going to where her father: King Percy is sitting. Keno is following close behind her. Ashley soon reaches her father's table.

Ashley – DAD!

King Percy – What is it sweety?

Ashley – Why were you trying to bribe Keno into staying away from me!?!

King Percy – Because he is not suited for you.

Ashley – What is that supposed to mean?

King Percy – He is not suitable for a princess. He's a poor simple man from another country. You shouldn't even be acquaintances with someone like him.

Ashley – But he is such a nice and kind person. I want to spend more time getting to know him. I want to see what a friendship with him might bring.

King Percy – Ashley, if you continue to see this boy than I will disown you and cut you off from all your financial and royal ties.

Ashley – What!?!

Scene 10

-Some time later, Keno and Ashley are again sitting next to one another at a table.

Ashley – I can't believe it Keno. My very own father is threatening to cut me out of his life if I continue seeing you.

Keno – Then leave him. You don't deserve to live with someone like that. Come back to where I live. You can stay with me or one of my friends. I think Kaitlyn's family has a spare room in their house. You can attend the same school as me. We can make this work.

Ashley – I don't know Keno. My father has always been in my life. I just can't walk away from him.

Keno – Ashley, your father is a discriminating fool!

Ashley – Keno, you can't call him... I mean... I... I need some time alone. Excuse me.

-Ashley quickly runs away as Keno simply sits still watching her run off.

Scene 11

-Some time later, Keno is still sitting at the same table. From nearby Jimmy walks over to Keno and sits down next to him.

Jimmy – So how long has Ashley been away from you?

Keno – According to my watch, about an hour. But it's felt like the longest hour of my life. In fact, this whole wedding has felt like the longest day of my life. Ugg. Why does trying to find the right girl for my life have to be so hard?

Jimmy – Keno, you just met her. How much progress did you really expect to make with this girl in just a day?

Keno – I just wanted to... start something. Something that with time could become something more and.. Err. But we have this driving force that's trying to keep us apart? Ugg. Why would God allow something this painful and confusing to happen to me?

Jimmy – Well maybe this is some way to keep you from jumping too soon into...

Keno – If you're trying to say that divine intervention is taking the form of a rude discriminating man, then just stop. I don't believe the Lord would create a road block in the form of something so wrong and...

Jimmy – Better hold that thought. Here comes Ashley.

-Keno turns his head and sees Ashley walking towards him.

Keno – Ashley.

Ashley – Keno, I've made a decision.

Keno – Yeah, and...

Ashely – I've decided we can't see each other anymore. I told my father that I was just coming to talk to you one more time. After that, he wants you and your friends to leave immediately.

Keno – Ashley, you can't give into your father. You have to stand firm on what you want and show him how you feel.

Ashley – Keno, we just met today. Is it right for us to fight so hard for this?

Keno – Is it right for us to be driven away due to a belief that is wrong? Is it right for us to be driven apart because of differences we can't help? We need to be strong and stay together.

Ashley – I'm sorry Keno but… I'm not strong enough to do that.

Keno – Yeah. I'm sorry too.

Ashley – I will miss you though.

-Both Keno and Ashley immediately hug one another.

Keno – I'll never forget you.

Ashley - And I'll never forget you.

-The two both take a moment to look at the other right in the eye and hold onto the other's hands. The two then slowly begin to move their bodies away from the other but still holding the other's hands. Then slowly the two let go of each other's hands and walk away in opposite directions.

Keno – It's time to go.

-Keno then begins to walk towards an exit door as from nearby both Jimmy and Kaitlyn follow close behind him.

Kaitlyn – Are you okay Keno?

Keno – No, I'm not okay. We both wanted to be together… but we can't. I guess this is just what life is supposed to be like for me. Constantly being unlucky in love.

Jimmy – Keno… this may be for the best.

Keno – Is it Jimmy? Maybe it is or maybe it isn't. I just don't see why God would allow this kind of painful heartbreak to happen to me though. Why? Why did it all have to happen like this!?

Jimmy – I don't know Keno. I don't know if being driven away from Ashley like the way you were is part of a good plan for your life, or if being driven away from Ashley like the way you were truly is a bad thing. But I know that whatever comes next, the Lord will take both the good and the bad things of your past and make something good happen for you in your future.

Keno – Hmm… Maybe… Come on guys. Let's go home.

THE END

Chapter 6 – Skipping Through Time

Scene 1

-In a high school laboratory, a teenage boy: Jimmy is working at a computer. He clicks and types quickly as his eyes are glued to the screen. From a nearby door, Jimmy's three friends: Keno, Kaitlyn, and Monica walk in.

Keno – Hey Jimmy. How are you doing?

Jimmy – Quite well. Making excellent progress today.

Monica – Well as the lead writer for the school newspaper, I would love to hear some details about this big new project of yours.

-Jimmy turns his head to look right at Monica.

Jimmy – Well you can't quote me officially for now, but I can reveal some details. I've created a machine that can allow you to see into the future.

Kaitlyn – Whoa. You mean you've created a time machine?

Jimmy – Not exactly. What I've really made is a machine that takes into account all of the parameters of what exists in reality and allows one to look through a window of what is probably to come in your future.

Monica – But a window can be broken. Is there anywhere someone could break that window and travel through it?

Jimmy – Unlikely but this technology is brand new. There's no telling what it's capable of doing. Which is why I need to perform tons of tests with it.

Keno – Well if it was anyone else I'd be worried, but I know you'll only use this technology for good.

Kaitlyn – Hey. We're going into town to grab some pizza and then do a babysitter's team up mission and take care of a whole bunch of kids in Keno's neighborhood together. Wanna come?

Jimmy – Well like I said, I need to perform a ton of tests on this new machine. We're talking major scientific progress here.

Kaitlyn – But Jimmy, you've spent the last few weeks barely talking to anybody. You've been spending every bit of your free time here.

Jimmy – And I'll spend the next few years in here if I have to if it means creating this new technology. Only I can perfect this technology to prevent any people with malicious intents from abusing my work.

Kaitlyn – But Jimmy, I really want to spend time with...

Keno – It's his choice Kaitlyn. Besides, I've learned that when it comes to creating new technology, the only person that can tear Jimmy away from his work is Jimmy himself.

Jimmy – Thanks for understanding. I'll see you guys later.

-Keno, Kaitlyn, and Monica prepare to leave the room. Kaitlyn looks back at Jimmy and calls out to him.

Kaitlyn – You can still join us if you change your mind. I know looking into the future is important, but don't forget about focusing on what's going on in the present.

-The three friends are soon all gone as Jimmy begins to open up a small mechanical device near him while he talks to himself.

Jimmy – Now where was I? Ah, yes. This is the trickiest part. This extremely rare element is what makes the change in chronoton particles possible. Now I just have to reverse the polarity of the neutron flow, but carefully. If I have these two wires cross then it could cause a huge electrical surge possibly causing the chronoton particles to create a surge of energy that...

-Suddenly Jimmy accidentally moves two small wires too close to one another. There is a spark that emits from the two wires and suddenly there is a huge white *FLASH!*

Scene 2

Monica – So who do you think we should do our history paper on?

-Jimmy looks around and sees he is in a classroom and realizes that he is sitting at a desk. Jimmy sees he is surrounded by Keno, Kaitlyn, and Monica while other groups of students are talking in the classroom.

Jimmy – Huh? What just happened?

Keno – Um, we're deciding on what famous person our group wants to do the biography project on. Where have you been?

Jimmy – In my lab. You guys just left after inviting me to have pizza and...

Kaitlyn – Jimmy, that was yesterday.

Monica – Yeah. What happened? Your brain so focused on your work you don't have any space left in your head for the other stuff you do in life?

Jimmy – No it's not that. I seriously recall working in my lab, accidentally moving two wires on my device to close to each other, there was a flash, and then I was in class.

Keno – Maybe this new technology you're working on has caused you to suffer some brain damage. Quick, tell me. What's your name? What grade did we meet? What period of the day is this?

Jimmy – My name is Jimmy. Keno, we met in second grade. And since we're in history class, this is seventh period. Look, I remember my entire life story. I just don't seem to recall the end of yesterday and the majority of today.

Kaitlyn – Well this sounds really weird. I mean you were working on technology that was supposed to help you see into the future. Not forget the past.

Jimmy – Wait a minute. Could it be that my device actually sent me into...

-FLASH!

Scene 3

Keno – Yeah. You were saying Jimmy... You just suddenly stopped talking mid-sentence there. Is everything okay?

-Jimmy turns his head and sees himself sitting across from Keno at a cafeteria table.

Jimmy – What just happened? I was talking with you, Kaitlyn, and Monica in history class about how I lost my memory of what happened over the last day and...

Keno – That weird moment? Jimmy that was last week. You acted weird for a minute, but then afterwards acted like everything was cool again. What's going on?

Jimmy – I... wait. You said that incident in history class happened last week. Which means that I've forgotten a whole week of my life now. Unless...

Keno – Unless what?

Jimmy – Unless my new technology has done more than open a window into the future. Chronoton particles are extremely unstable and unpredictable at times. It could be that instead of allowing me to open up a window through time and space, the unstable particles have allowed my mind to move through time and space.

Keno – But you were sitting right in front of me this whole time. How could you come here from the past when you were already here?

Jimmy – My body has remained stable but not my brain. Apparently the device has relocated my brain patterns. Causing me to view my own personal future not through a window, but through my own body. Either I'm actually in the future, or the device is causing me to see a virtual projection of the future that I can interact with, or maybe an electrical surge knocked me out and I'm dreaming, or this is a virtual projection of the future that's being projected into my brain through a dream.

Keno – It all just sounds confusing to me. But how are you going to get your brain back to normal?

Jimmy – We have to use the technology in my lab. It's the only way to fix this. Come on. I might need a little help.

-Keno and Jimmy both get up and begin walking out of the cafeteria. As they begin to walk in the hallway they are spotted by Kaitlyn.

Kaitlyn – Oh hey Jimmy. I was wondering if we could maybe have some lunch together and...

Jimmy – No time Kaitlyn. Work to be done. I need to...

-FLASH!

Scene 4

Kaitlyn – I'll wait Jimmy! I'll wait!

-Jimmy looks through the window of a bus as he sees Kaitlyn waving to him from a sidewalk. The bus Jimmy is sitting in is starting to drive away. Jimmy turns his head to look at the passengers around him. He then begins to quickly look through a bag that is near his feet.

Jimmy – These are a bunch of my prized possessions. The only reason I would be carrying all of these with me though is if I was... moving.

-Jimmy then quickly gets out of his pocket: a cell phone, and begins dialing a number.

Jimmy – Come on Keno. Please tell me you haven't changed your phone number.

-Jimmy then hears Keno's voice answer the phone.

Keno – Hello. Keno here.

Jimmy – Keno, its Jimmy.

Keno – Hey Jimmy. Calling right after the big goodbye we had an hour ago. What happened? You forget something at the school you want me to go back for? I thought you cleared your whole lab out after graduation.

Jimmy – Graduation? You mean high school graduation?

Keno – Yeah. You remember? Our high school graduation you experienced this morning.

Jimmy – To be honest, I don't remember Keno. Apparently I've just experienced over two years of a jump in my life.

Keno – Wait. You're starting to act like you did years ago when you claimed that your brain was jumping through time or something like that.

Jimmy – Yes. Did I make any progress in figuring out what was happening to me at any point before today?

Keno – Well to be honest, you kind of gave up your research in that area a long time ago. Said you weren't making any progress. You decided to look into different projects. Kaitlyn was happy at first because she thought that meant you would dedicate more time to being with her.

Jimmy – And did I?

Keno – Well at the end of graduation, both of you did sort of promise to the other that one day you would both get...

-FLASH!

Scene 5

Kaitlyn – It sure feels amazing to be married doesn't it?

-Jimmy notices he is sitting on the couch of an unfamiliar house with Kaitlyn sitting very close to him. Jimmy scoots quickly away from Kaitlyn with a very confused look on his face.

Jimmy – Ahh! Married!?! What's going on? I had just graduated from high school! When did this happen?

Kaitlyn – I know. It feels like just yesterday that we graduated from high school. But when you know that one day you're going to be with the person you love, eight years can go by very quickly.

Jimmy – Eight years!?

Kaitlyn – Jimmy, you suddenly look like you're really out of place. What's wrong?

Jimmy – Kaitlyn, remember back in high school when I claimed to suddenly forget about what had been happening to me recently and that my brain might be jumping through time. Well it's continuing to happen. Only this time, after seeing a short bit of my life after high school graduation, I'm now suddenly here.

Kaitlyn – Oh my. It's happening. Keno told me to be ready for this day.

-Kaitlyn quickly takes out a cell phone and dials a number.

Kaitlyn – Keno, its Kaitlyn. Jimmy has suddenly claimed to have come from the past. Get here now!

-Kaitlyn quickly hangs up the phone and looks at Jimmy.

Kaitlyn – As crazy as your story back in the day sounded, Keno was convinced you of all people would have had the ability to send your young mind into the future. So Keno made sure that you built a machine to analyze you the next time your mind jumps through time so that we can find some way to send your young mind into the past and fix all of this.

Jimmy – Wow. Good to know you guys still care. So I guess we now wait for Keno to get here with the machine. But while we're waiting... you said it's been eight years and we're married now.

Kaitlyn – Well... yes. We're married.

Jimmy – Wow. So... how long has it been since the wedding?

Kaitlyn – Just two weeks.

Jimmy – Wait. It took me eight years to ask you to marry me?

Kaitlyn – Not exactly. We had both made a... commitment when we graduated from high school. You promised we would get married once you had gotten your master's degree and made some great scientific breakthrough to help the world.

Jimmy – And apparently I did?

Kaitlyn – Yes. There are just times that I wish during that eight years you had... taken a break to spend more time with me. But when I was young once, I dreamed about a life where we didn't end up together. And I never want that life to happen to me for real. So I was willing to wait as long as it would take for us to finally be together.

Jimmy – Whoa. That's...

-Keno suddenly runs in through the door with a type of small scanner machine.

Keno – Activating now.

Jimmy – Hey Keno. Whoa. You've aged a bit.

Keno – Yes I have. Now stand still Jimmy. We're probably almost out of time. We have to make sure this machine gets a real detailed scan of you before...

-FLASH!

Scene 6

Young Girl – Are you my dad?

-Jimmy finds himself standing in a large auditorium with a young girl standing right near him, looking up at his face.

Jimmy – Huh? What?

-From nearby Kaitlyn walks over to Jimmy.

Kaitlyn – Come on Jimmy. Having trouble recognizing your own daughter?

Jimmy – What!? My daughter!

Kaitlyn – Oh no. Could it… Jimmy. Do you remember what's occurred over the last ten years?

Jimmy – It's been ten years?!!

Kaitlyn – This doesn't seem like a false alarm. Keno, get over here! Terra, go play with Miss Monica and Jenny.

-Kaitlyn pushes the young girl away while Keno rushes over.

Kaitlyn – Keno, operation mind jump is on.

Keno – To my office, move quickly.

-Keno leads Jimmy and Kaitlyn quickly out of the auditorium and into an office. Keno quickly opens a safe and from it, takes out the small scanner machine. Keno presses a few buttons on it and then points it at Jimmy.

Keno – Okay. I've set the machine to lock into your brain patterns Jimmy. According to you when you helped build this, the next time your mind jumps through time, it should take you back to the location your brain patterns originated from… maybe.

Jimmy – What do you mean maybe?

Keno – Well it's like you said back in high school. You aren't sure how this is happening. It could be time travel or it could be some weird projection you're trapped in. Either way, this is the only plan we've got.

Jimmy – So… we just wait to see if it works?

Keno – Pretty much.

Jimmy – So… what's been going on in the ten years since I last saw you both?

Keno – Well me and Monica restarted the after school care club this building used to house when we were young. We've been open for over ten years now and have done a lot of good in…

Kaitlyn – You know Keno, I think Jimmy is more interested in what me and him have been up to.

Keno – Oh… right.

Jimmy – So… I have a daughter?

Kaitlyn – Yeah. Terra… she's amazing.

Jimmy – I'll bet. But why did she ask me if I'm her father? Wouldn't she recognize me easily?

-Keno and Kaitlyn both glance at the other and then tilt their heads down.

Jimmy – What? What's gone wrong? Kaitlyn, are we divorced or…

Kaitlyn – No, no, no! We've been married for eighteen years now and the only women you ever look at are me and our daughter… but…

Jimmy – But what? What kind of action have I done that I…

Kaitlyn – That's just it. You haven't taken any action. You're always so absorbed in your work. Between work at the university and building the next great invention, you never have time for me, and barely even look at your daughter. I mean, Keno has to pick up your slack in parenting.

Keno – Kaitlyn, maybe you shouldn't…

Kaitlyn – No Keno. You've never heard me say these exact words, and you need to hear it at the same time as him. Jimmy, Keno has been more of a father to Terra than you have. He helps her with her homework, plays games with her, was a tremendous help when Terra was going through a period of depression, and...

Jimmy – Wait. My daughter was dealing with depression?

Kaitlyn – Yes! And that was in part because she believed her father didn't love her. She knew you were still married to me and was always somewhere not far away, but was confused why you never had time for her. And Keno helped her through it. He has a real knack at bonding with and helping fatherless children in the community and that's what Terra has become. A fatherless child.

Jimmy – Listen. If Terra is important to me then I'm sure...

-FLASH!

Scene 7

Terra – It's your fault mom is sick!

-Jimmy finds himself standing in a hospital hallway with a grown up version of his daughter Terra standing in front of him.

Jimmy – Oh no. The scanner device didn't work. I'm still jumping through time and... Wait. Kaitlyn is sick?

Terra – Yeah dad. That's why we're in a hospital. You're just starting to realize that reality exists beyond your work? Like the part where for the last thirty years, you had a family?

Jimmy – Wait. What's been happening to Kaitlyn? How long...

Terra – You would have known months ago if you had actually come home to do more than sleep occasionally. You would've noticed the symptoms immediately and maybe have developed some kind of way to cure her.

Jimmy – Terra, I'm scientifically proficient but I'm not a medical doctor. I don't know how to...

Terra – You create new technology after new technology all of the time. You could've made something to help mom long ago. When you put your mind to it, you can create anything you want.... except some way to save your family.

Jimmy – Terra, listen. It's hard to explain but I've been...

Terra – A bad father. I know. You've made that apology before and it's getting old. You know, I barely saw you at all as a child. There were a couple of times when on a rare occurrence, you would pick me up from after care and I wouldn't even recognize you. It was like you were some time traveler. Constantly jumping forward through time. Staying just long enough for me to catch a glimpse of you before you went away for another long time jump.

Jimmy – Exactly. Terra, a piece of technology I was working on caused...

Terra – Yes, all of that great technology; all of those great projects you worked on since you were in high school. So was it worth it dad? Was all of that time in your life you lost to your work worth it?

Jimmy – Terra. Listen. You need to know that...

-FLASH!

Scene 8

-Jimmy suddenly finds himself on his knees at a cemetery. Jimmy turns his head and sees Kaitlyn's name on one tomb stone. He turns his head and sees Terra's name another tomb stone. Jimmy's head nearly comes to the ground and he hits the ground with his two fists.

Jimmy – Kaitlyn... and my daughter... No! My entire family... my life... I barely had a chance with them... it just flashed by before I could...

-Suddenly Jimmy's thoughts are interrupted as he begins to hear voices.

Kaitlyn's Voice – Jimmy!

-Jimmy looks up at the sky seeing nobody.

Jimmy – Kaitlyn! Is that you?

Keno's Voice – Hey Jimmy!

Jimmy – Keno?

Monica's Voice – Jimmy, wake up!

Jimmy – What?

Kaitlyn's Voice – Wake up Jimmy!

-FLASH!

Scene 9

Keno – He's opening his eyes!

-Jimmy slowly begins to sit up as he sees that he is on the floor of the high school laboratory. Surrounding him are Keno, Kaitlyn, and Monica.

Jimmy – Guys. What's going on?

Monica – As we were leaving, we saw a flash come from your lab. We came back and saw you were lying on the floor asleep.

Keno – Your pulse and vitals seemed normal but we've been trying to wake you up for the last two minutes. Just to make sure you still had brain activity or weren't going through a seizure or something like that.

Jimmy – Two minutes? But it feels so much longer.

Kaitlyn – What do you mean? Did you have a little dream while you were out cold?

Jimmy – Yeah… maybe. Could it have been a dream or could my machine have really worked?

Keno – What do you mean?

Jimmy – My machine that can allow one to see into the future. I was working on it before there was a flash and I… during the two minutes I was asleep, my mind may have been projected into the future which my brain could only comprehend by making my body fall asleep and interpret as a dream. If that's the case then I may have accidently had the breakthrough that I need to…

-Jimmy suddenly begins to stop talking as he starts to look right at Kaitlyn's face. He's silent for a moment but then begins to speak again.

Jimmy – Or maybe it was just a dream. I have been working hard. I think I need a real long break. Hey. Is that offer for pizza still on?

Kaitlyn – Yeah, you bet it is. You wanna help us babysit too?

Jimmy – Well... sure. You know there's no point in building new technology if you don't help take care of the next generation that's gonna use it.

Kaitlyn – Allright. Here. Let me help you up.

-Kaitlyn holds out her hand and she helps Jimmy stand up. Once the two are both standing up, for one moment: both Jimmy and Kaitlyn find themselves staring into one another's eyes. The two smile.

Jimmy – Allright then. Let's move forward with our lives guys.

-Keno and Monica both begin to walk out of the laboratory while Jimmy and Kaitlyn both follow closely behind them. Then as Jimmy and Kaitlyn each use a hand to close the door to the laboratory, they both soon find those same hands holding on to the others' as they move forward together.

THE END

Chapter 7 – Miscommunication

Hey Mr. Lee! I put a lot of work into this original story. So please give me an "A"!!! Please, please, please! ☺

*Kaitlyn Krammer
ENG10, Period 7
Original Story Project*

Miscommunication

Scene 1

-A large group of teenage students are sitting in their public school classroom. Their male teacher stands in front of the class and begins to speak to them.

Mr. Parry: All right students. Quiet down, quiet down. Now recently in class we've been talking about the meaning of communication. But today I want to talk you all about what miscommunication is. Now miscommunication is basically when a message isn't transmitted from one person to another properly. It could happen due to not enough information being given, the party receiving the information adds manufactured details to the facts, and/or words are simply misheard.

-Suddenly a female teacher walks into the room.

Miss Lynn: Mr. Parry. I'm here to sub for you now.

Mr. Parry: Ah, Miss Lynn. Come in. Now students, I have to go to a conference now but Miss Lynn will be here to substitute. Behave. Remember students. Behavior is an important principle.

-Mr. Parry then leaves the room and the students begin to whisper to one another.

Student 1: What he say?

Student 2: Something about how if we behave he'll become a principal.

Scene 2

-The sound of a school bell running is heard. Students begin to walk through the hallway and talk with one another.

Student 3: So what was it that Mr. Parry said before he left?

Student 4: Something about how if we behave he'll have to take lynthenol.

Student 5: What is that? Some type of new medication?

Student 6: Did you say Mr. Parry is on medication?

Scene 3

-At a mall, a young teenage boy is walking around with a smile on his face.

Student 7: Ah. I love hanging out at the mall.

-Suddenly, a cell phone ring tone is heard. The teenager takes out their cell phone and begins talking to their friend on the other line.

Student 7: Hello?

Student 6: Hey Brian, its John. Did ya here? Mr. Parry is taking some new medication. It must mean all of the teachers are getting sick.

Student 7: Whoa. Far out. Well I'll talk to you later.

-Student 7 walks around again, and then after a moment, the sound of a cell phone is heard again. He quickly answers it and begins talking to another friend.

Student 7: Hello?

Roger: Hey Brian. It's ya pal Roger. How are things goin with you?

Student 7: Okay, but did you hear? There's an epidemic at school that's got all of the teachers.

Roger: Whoa! That's big. Well I'll talk to you later Brian.

-The teenager begins to walk forward but within seconds, the cell phone is heard again. The teenager quickly answers it.

Student 7: Hello? (frustrated that's he's answered his cell phone many times now)

Roger: Brian, it's Roger again. What does "epidemic" mean?

Student 7: (sarcastically) It's a synonym for alien invasion. What else would it be? Now I'm turning off my phone.

-The teenager quickly turns their cell phone off.

Student 7: Ugg. He's how old and he doesn't know what epidemic means? Sheesh.

Scene 4

-Roger is now standing before an army of over one hundred teenagers that are all starting to listen to him speak.

Roger: Fellow students! I have from a reliable source, that aliens have invaded our school and have captured all of our teachers!

Skeptic Teenager 1: Why should we believe you?

Skeptic Teenager 2: Yes. This just sounds crazy.

Roger: It is not crazy. The aliens are here! And if we don't stop them, they'll take everything we hold close and dear.

Skeptic Teenager 3: You're just talking crazy.

Roger: My fellow students! Listen to me! You all may think this is all fake but I assure you good children it is real. You may think - The aliens aren't real. We have peace, peace. But I assure you the aliens are real and there is no peace. The intergalactic war has actually begun. The next fleet that sweeps from space will bring to our ears the clash of resounding phasers. Our teachers are already captured. Why stand we here idle? What is it that children wish? What would they have? Is life so dear or peace so sweet as to be purchased at the price of chains of slavery? Forbid it Almighty God! I know not what course others may take, but as for me, give me pizza or give me death!

-Moved by Roger's speech, all of the teenagers begin to scream like crazy army soldiers.

Roger: Onward to victory. Raaaaahhh!

-Suddenly Mr. Parry appears and walks over to the group of teenagers.

Mr. Parry: Hey. What are all you kids doing!?

Roger: Mr. Parry. How did you escape from the aliens?

Mr. Parry: What aliens?

Roger: Well we heard aliens abducted you and all of the teachers.

Mr. Parry: What gave you that crazy idea? It sounds like some sort of miscommunication happened somewhere. Now then. I'll see you all tomorrow.

-Mr. Parry then walks away.

Random Student 1: So does this mean we're not going to fight aliens?

Random Student 2: But we're so hyped up. Let's go fight someone anyway. What do you think Roger?

Roger: Hold on. Let me put on my glasses. Ah hem. My friends, you must pardon me. I have grown older in your service and now find myself going crazy.

-Roger then slowly walks away.

Random Student 3: This has to be the weirdest day I've ever had.

THE END!

Chapter 8 - Arlene

Scene 1

-A school bell rings, and soon after: hundreds of teenagers are walking out of a high school building. Walking together are the three teenagers: Keno, Jimmy, and Kaitlyn.

Kaitlyn – I am just so glad all of that testing is over. Well, there's my ride. See ya Keno.

Keno – See ya Kaitlyn.

Kaitlyn – Um… bye Jimmy.

Jimmy – Oh, bye.

-Jimmy quickly holds out a hand to give Kaitlyn a high five while Kaitlyn holds out her arms showing that she's ready for a hug. The two both notice what the other is doing and Jimmy quickly switches his arms to show he's ready for a hug while Kaitlyn switches to showing that she's ready to give a high five. The two's faces turn red.

Kaitlyn – Okay. Bye.

-Kaitlyn quickly walks away while Jimmy walks in another direction with his face still red.

Keno – Dude, when are you going to just ask her out? You both just can't keep acting awkward about it.

Jimmy – It's... difficult. Technology and school work I get but... this... there's just so many unknown variables to work with. It's not easy for me.

Keno – Well you and Kaitlyn need to come to an understanding sooner than later. You both have been real awesome at helping me through my... difficulties, when it's come to my relationships. I just wanna see you two make this work before something bad might happen that might shake up what's between you two...

-Suddenly from nearby, a teenage girl runs over to Jimmy and immediately hugs him.

Arlene – JIMMY!!!

Jimmy – Whoa! Um... hi there.

Keno – So Jimmy... who is this?

Jimmy – Oh, Keno. This is Arlene. She used to go to school with me when we were little but she moved away at the end of first grade, just before I met you.

Arlene – And you look so much like you did when you were little. It's like you've become a tall version of the amazing boy I once knew.

Keno – So it sounds like you both knew each other well.

Arlene – And we still do. Besides, I'm Jimmy's girlfriend.

Keno – What!?

-Jimmy sighs as he closes his eyes.

Jimmy – It's... kind of true.

Scene 2

-At a playground: Keno, Jimmy and Arlene are all sitting on separate swings next to each other as the three talk.

Arlene – It was young love when it happened. We had known each other since preschool. We always spent our time together. Eventually we became very good friends. Always hanging out at the others' house. We ended up holding hands all of the time.

Keno – So that's how she became your girlfriend?

Jimmy – Look. We weren't exactly a couple. Before she moved away, we made a silly promise at the playground one day that we would one day get married and..

Arlene – And I've been waiting patiently since then for the day where we could finally be together again. As soon as my parents said I was old enough to travel on my own, I knew that this was the first place that I had to visit.

Keno – So how did you know where to find Jimmy if you both haven't seen each other since first grade?

Jimmy – We've been pen pals since then, writing letters and eventually sending e-mails backs and forth.

Arlene – It's been a proper substitute that kept me decently happy until the day where we could finally be reunited. Just like old times.

Jimmy – Arlene, we've been nothing but pen pals for a decade. You can't just expect to come back here on a vacation and think things are going to be like the way they were when you left.

Arlene – But I'm sure if we try, we can make it like old times.

Jimmy – That's the thing though. We can't. Things have changed. Things have...

Kaitlyn's Voice – Jimmy!

-The three turn their heads and see Kaitlyn running towards them. Jimmy immediately gets up to greet Kaitlyn.

Jimmy – Kaitlyn, hey.

Kaitlyn – Hey Jimmy. Someone said they saw you heading over here. I forgot to give you back your calculator that you loaned me. Thank you by the way.

-Kaitlyn hands Jimmy a calculator.

Jimmy – Oh, it's cool. You're welcome.

-Jimmy again quickly holds out a hand to give Kaitlyn a high five while Kaitlyn holds out her arms showing that she's ready for a hug. The two both notice what the other is doing and Jimmy quickly switches his arms to show he's ready for a hug while Kaitlyn switches to showing that she's ready to give a high five. The two's faces turn red.

Kaitlyn – Well I have to go.

-Kaitlyn begins to turn around but her foot gets caught on a root coming out of the ground and she begins to trip and fall down.

Kaitlyn – Ahh!

Jimmy – Kaitlyn!

-Jimmy moves quickly and catches Kaitlyn before she hits the ground. Jimmy now holds Kaitlyn in his arms and the two suddenly find themselves looking at the other's face. The two's faces instantly turn red.

Kaitlyn – Thank you... again.

Jimmy – You're welcome... again.

-Jimmy then helps Kaitlyn stand up as the two continue to look at the other.

Kaitlyn – Well... like I already said... I have to go... but before I go, I hope you don't mind if I...

-Kaitlyn quickly moves her face forward and kisses Jimmy's cheek. After a moment: Kaitlyn backs up, turns around, and quickly runs away. Jimmy touches his cheek as he smiles. Meanwhile near him, Arlene is still sitting on the swing and has watched everything that just occurred. Arlene turns her face away with a look of worry on her face.

Scene 3

-On an outdoor balcony attached to Jimmy's house, both Jimmy and Arlene are standing alone. The two look up at the night sky as they walk.

Jimmy – Man. It sure is a beautiful night.

Arlene – It is. So... Keno tells me that you and that girl Kaitlyn have been friends for a long time... and you never told me about her in any of your letters or e-mails. Why is that?

Jimmy – Well you see Arlene... you're my friend, and a good one at that. But I don't tell you everything about my life. No one reveals every detail of what they do and who their friends are in letters or e-mails. Kaitlyn is just one of those details I didn't see a point in sharing.

Arlene – But it's not like you to withhold from me stuff about your friends. We used to tell each other everything. I mean... remember when we were in preschool and we would always take a nap next to each other. We would never sleep. We would just talk. And we became such close friends. Remember in first grade when we walked from lunch to recess. We'd always hold hands. Back then boys and girls wouldn't get along. They'd bug us for holding hands but we didn't care. It didn't bother either of us. I just came back this weekend so we could relive those times. So we could hold hands again, talk, and act like nothing had happened since I left.

Jimmy – That's just it though. Lots of things have happened since you left. Look, I'll admit. During the first few years after you moved away, I did wish we could relive those old times. Whenever I was having a rough time, I imagined you were still with me, and I would pretend I was still talking to you. But things changed. There's a reason why things can't be the way they used to be.

Arlene – Then can you tell me what that reason is?

Jimmy – I... I can't Arlene.

Arlene – Well... if that's the way you want to be, then I'll go now.

-Arlene begins to walk down a set of steps attached to the balcony.

Jimmy – Wait Arlene. I didn't mean it that way!

-Without saying anything, Arlene walks away. Jimmy tilts his head down low.

Jimmy – Well... I really messed that up.

Scene 4

-The next day, Arlene stands by herself at a bus stop. She briefly glances at her watch as she talks to herself.

Arlene – Hmm. The bus must be running a bit late.

Jimmy's Voice – Arlene! Wait!!!

-Arlene turns her head and sees Jimmy running up to her. Jimmy stops to catch his breath and then talks to her.

Jimmy – Okay. The reason why I was acting so weird and indirect with you is because... I'm in love with Kaitlyn.

Arlene – Hmm. Well it's about time you admitted it.

Jimmy – Huh? You knew?

Arlene – Of course I did. In fact, even before I came here, I could tell by the way you were writing your e-mails that your mind was elsewhere. I really just came to see if your heart truly was with somebody else or if there was still some chance it was connected to me. Apparently it isn't.

Jimmy – So you're not mad?

Arlene – I'm only mad that you didn't admit it to me immediately. Hey, it's all okay. This kind of stuff happens. I shouldn't have expected things to be like they were when we were little.

-The two then notice a bus pulling up near them.

Arlene – Well, that would be my bus. Gotta go.

Jimmy – Yeah. Goodbye Arlene.

Arlene – Goodbye Jimmy.

-Arlene turns, preparing herself to get on the bus. She then turns to look at Jimmy one more time.

Arlene – Hey Jimmy! If you finally work up the nerve to tell Kaitlyn *herself* how you feel, and she tells you that she likes you back... tell her that I said she's one real lucky girl.

-Arlene waves and then walks onto the bus. Soon after, the bus drives away. Jimmy smiles as he begins to get out a cell phone. Jimmy dials a number and soon begins talking into the phone.

Jimmy – Kaitlyn? Hey, it's Jimmy. You free to meet up some time today? There's something important that I want to tell you.

THE END

Chapter 9 – The Not So Perfect Life

Scene 1

-In a simple town, an eighteen year old girl named Monica walks down a sidewalk with a smile on her face. Her smile begins to fade though as she sees three police cars with flashing lights parked right next to her house. Monica's face becomes more worried and she begins to walk faster as she sees two police officers talking with her father right outside the front door of the house. Monica rushes over to her father interrupting a conversation he was having with the police officers.

Monica *– Dad. What's going on? Where's mom?*

-Monica's dad stands silent, eyes turned slightly away from Monica with an expression indicating that he's unsure of what to say. Monica's face becomes more worried.

Monica *– Dad. Where's mom!?!*

-Outside of an elementary school, a twenty two year old woman named Monica walks down a sidewalk with an upset look on her face. As she walks forward, Monica holds a purse in her left hand as she digs into the purse with her right hand. Within seconds Monica pulls out a badge with her name and a photo of herself on it. Monica attaches the badge to a necklace and puts it around her neck as she speaks softly to herself.

Monica – There. I've got the name badge on today. Now I've got the complete work attire on.

-Monica walks through the front door of the elementary school. Monica immediately turns left heading towards the school cafeteria. Immediately as she enters through the cafeteria doors she sees a room full of about fifty students sitting in metal chairs watching two students standing at podiums talking. Immediately a young male adult named Subin walks next to Monica and looks at her.

Subin – Hey Monica. The fifth grade students are having their student class presidential debate and election today. So we have to wait for them to be done before we can set up.

-Monica stands with a slightly upset face as she rolls her eyes.

Monica – Don't these school leaders know it takes more than a minute to convert a cafeteria into an after school care organization? They can't keep doing these late afternoon events in the cafeteria every day.

Subin – Hey. We'll have enough time to set up. We always do. Let's just watch this debate for now.

-Monica turns to watch the talking students more closely as she begins to speak softly to herself.

Monica – What's the point of teaching these students about debates and elections? They're never run fairly anyway.

-A nineteen year old Monica sits in front of the television in the living room of her house. As Monica looks closely at the television, she listens to two news casters talk.

News Caster 1 – *And so with 94 percent of the votes, Robert Daves is voted out of the mayor's office today and will soon be replaced by reigning champion of the polls: Jaden Lennox.*

News Caster 2 – *As most viewers know, this election was brought about after a petition was created with the highest number of signatures in our town's history due to a loss in confidence in Robert Dave's leadership ability.*

News Caster 1 – *This loss of confidence occurred a year ago shortly after Robert Dave's wife: Marla Daves died due to drug overdose. She was found dead when...*

-The television is suddenly turned off. Monica turns her head to see her father standing behind her with a television remote in his hand.

Monica's Father – *You really don't need to watch that. I already got the news myself three hours ago.*

Monica – *It isn't fair dad. You know that.*

Monica's Father – *That's politics Monica. When you're associated with individuals who partake in illegal activity, people get worried that you might be partaking in the same illegal activity.*

Monica – *Mom wasn't your second in command in office or something like that. She was your wife. It's not like you were taking drugs with her.*

Monica' Father – *Well I sure didn't do the best job at stopping her from taking them.*

Monica – *Neither of us knew she was...*

Monica's Father – *Let's be real Monica. We both had our suspicions. And I shouldn't have married someone that smokes to begin with. I'm sorry about all of this sweety. I'm sorry my mistakes have led you to losing so much.*

Monica – *Dad. I'm sure you'll find a new job.*

Monica's Father – *No. I'm sorry you didn't get accepted into any of those law schools you were interested in... again.*

Monica – *It's... it's no big...*

Monica's Father – *Yes it is Monica. I'm sorry.*

Monica – I'm glad you've said sorry. Now pick up those blocks.

-In the elementary school cafeteria, Monica stands as she watches three young boys pick up several blocks on the floor and put them back into a container. With a simple yet satisfied look on her face, Monica goes to sit down with several fifth grade students that are all drawing and coloring pictures with pencils and markers. Monica notices a fifth grade girl named Madison drawing a picture.

Monica – Hey Madison. What's that you're drawing there?

Madison – It's a picture for career day on Friday. We're supposed to draw a picture and write about what kind of job we want to do when we grow up.

Monica – So why are you drawing so many fish then?

Madison – I've told you before Miss Monica. It's because I want to be a marine biologist when I grow up.

Monica – Sorry. I keep forgetting that because your art work is always so good, I keep assuming you're going to be some great artist when you grow up.

-Suddenly a short first grade girl with long hair named Sami rushes over to the two wearing a lab coat.

Sami – Hey Miss Monica. Look at my cool lab coat I'm gonna wear for career day on Friday.

Monica – A lab coat huh? So are you gonna be a scientist when you grow up?

Sami – Yeah.

Monica – So what kind of a scientist?

Sami – The kind of scientist that mixes chemicals together and blows things up!

Monica – Oh… um…. that's…. well… okay.

Sami – Yep. That's what I'm gonna do when I grow up. So what are you gonna do when you grow up Miss Monica?

Madison – Sami, Miss Monica's already grown up. So she's already doing what she wanted to do when she grew up.

Sami – But maybe this isn't what she wanted to do.

Monica – *This isn't what I wanted!*

-In a small office, a twenty year old Monica sits across from a well-dressed man named Mr. Matthews at a desk.

Mr. Matthews – *I'm sorry Monica but you will not be receiving the Star Scholarship this year. You can however still attempt to…*

Monica – *I don't want your pamphlets about other scholarships as if they're consolation prizes. I've been rejected for every scholarship I've applied to within this organization.*

Mr. Matthews – *I'm sorry Monica but we can only give a limited number of scholarships per year to individuals with outstanding…*

Monica – *I was the top of my class in high school! I've got letters or recommendation from prestigious law firms I interned in! How much more outstanding can you get!?!*

Mr. Matthews – *Look Monica. Your academic performance is above average but the board is hesitant to give scholarships to those with close ties to individuals that have controversial backgrounds.*

Monica – *By individuals you mean my drug overdosed mother. I already subjected myself to your stupid drug tests every year when I applied for these scholarships, and every year I come out clean. I'm not a drug attic like my mother!*

Mr. Matthews – *I'm aware Monica but listen…*

Monica – *No! You listen. My dad chose to marry my mother so I sort of understand why the public wanted him out of office. However I was **born** into my family. I didn't choose to have close ties with my mother: the individual that has a controversial background.*

Mr. Matthews – *Now Monica. We're not the only organization that provides scholarships to…*

Monica – *You're the only organization that provides scholarships to the law schools I wanted to attend. Even still, no one else is helping me out. Look, with the money that both my dad and I have, I can only attend community college part time. And even if I wanted to take law classes there, there are many prerequisite courses I have to take first. And at the rate I'm going, by the time I take all those* *prerequisite courses and get to the real law classes, the prerequisite list may change and I may not be admitted into those classes and maybe even have to start all over.*

Mr. Matthews – *Then you may have to settle on working full time and build up enough funds before you attempt going back to school.*

Monica – *You don't think I know that? I've applied to tons of government jobs and law firms but they're even less helpful than you.*

Mr. Matthews – *Then you're going to have to cast your net wider Monica. Apply for types of jobs that you would have never normally applied for.*

Madison – Of course this is a job she wanted Sami. That's why she chose to work here.

-Monica sits at the cafeteria table with an expression that indicates she's unsure of what to say next while Madison and Sami look at her.

Madison – Come on Miss Monica. Tell Sami. Isn't this the job you wanted? Isn't this the most perfect place to be?

Monica – Well... you guys are fun but things are... well... my life is not so perfect... but... Hey wait. Sami. What's that picture you're drawing?

-Sami holds up a crude drawing with lots of colors and lines all over it.

Sami – It's my picture of a post-zombie apocalypse. See, the zombies are having a war with the gummy bears and the unicorns. See here. The zombie just took off the head of the gummy bear and is using it as a bowling ball to take down the unicorns.

Monica – That's just... wow. Sami, where you get your inspiration?

-Sami stares at her art work for a moment, then she tilts her head up and speaks an answer.

Sami – HAPPY MEALS!

-Monica sits quiet for a moment. Then she bursts out into laughter.

Scene 2

-Monica walks away from the elementary school with a slight smile on her face as she speaks softly to herself.

Monica – That girl is crazy. Sometimes I wonder if she's either mentally insane or one of the greatest young comedic geniuses ever.

-Suddenly a figure begins to appear from behind a dark corner of the school and a voice is heard.

Voice – I know *you're* a genius Miss Daves.

-Monica turns her head to see the unknown figure in the dark corner show themselves.

Monica – And who are you?

-The figure comes into the light to show them self to be a 40 year old man in a black suit. The man pulls a badge out of his pocket and immediately shows it Monica. The first words that grab Monica's attention are the name – Charles Avery, and the acronym – FBI.

Charles – I'm agent Charles Avery of the FBI. If you need further proof of my identity I can...

Monica – My dad used to be the mayor. Just like he needed to, he made sure I could quickly distinguish between real and fake ID's. Now let's cut the chase. What do you want from me? I've already had tons of private and public investigators approach me over the years trying to get "the real truth" about my family. Not that you all didn't milk enough real *and* fake facts out of us.

Charles – You misunderstand my intentions Miss Daves. I'm not here to question you. I'm here to recruit you.

Monica – You what?

Charles – Like you're aware, you were the top of your high school graduating class and did impressive work during your internships in multiple law firms. The investigative work you provided to your mentor lawyers provided them tremendous assistance when they represented their clients in courts. Your efforts did not go unnoticed.

Monica – Doesn't keep people from assuming that I must be the spawn of Satin though.

Charles – Your mother's background means little to us Miss Daves. The FBI is concerned with examining new recruit's current capabilities, not their family back stories.

Monica – So wait. You're saying you actually want to... recruit me into the FBI?

Charles – Yes. We've already checked into every drug and background test you've ever subjected yourself to. Plus, your current life situation makes you perfect recruit material.

Monica – What do you mean my current life situation?

Charles – Many people we attempt to recruit into the FBI have already obtained very ideal life situations. Prestigious jobs, ideal families, and/or all around seemingly perfect lives. But your life is nowhere near perfect Miss Daves. Your family is broken, the only job you can get is working part time with children; essentially: your life is not perfect. Meaning you have very little to lose by abandoning what you have and come work for us.

Monica – Look. This is all just...

Charles – Please Miss Daves. Your country needs you. This is your opportunity to have a job that is truly worthy of a woman of your skills. This is your opportunity to have a perfect life again.

Scene 3

-In a small hallway located in the middle of her home, Monica pushes a detailed drawing of a flower against the wall with one hand, while she uses the other hand to pin the paper to the wall with four thumb tacks. As Monica completes her assignment, her father walks into the hallway and immediately sees what Monica is doing.

Monica's Father – Another picture? Monica, you've got to stop hanging up all of these pictures your students give you.

Monica – But its good art dad. How can I not hang it up?

Monica's Father – You know you're making me look bad Monica.

Monica – How so?

Monica's Father – Whenever you gave me art work when you were a child, I just put it in a drawer. When your students give you art work, you hang it up in prestigious fashion. You must really love those kids of yours.

Monica – They're all right. Oh, did I tell you about this really funny thing one of my students said to me today?

Monica's Father – In a text message you sent me immediately after the student said it. By the way, I thought you weren't supposed to use your phone while at work.

Monica – Well... I... um...

Monica Father – Hey. It's okay Monica. I'm glad you're enjoying your job. I know it wasn't your first choice of workplace but...

Monica – It's not perfect but I'm dealing.

-Monica's father smiles and begins to walk away. He stops as Monica begins to speak again.

Monica - Dad... do you ever wonder... like... how life could be different?

Monica's Father – Different in what way?

Monica – Like what if mom had never started taking any drugs or what if you were still the town mayor. Like... what if our lives were still perfect. Stuff like that.

Monica's Father – To be honest, sometimes I do. However I've started to realize that in this world, sometimes good things *can* be born from the worst circumstances.

Monica – Hmm. Maybe.

Monica's Father – Now then. Are you about ready for dinner?

Monica – Yeah. Oh, let me say it now before I forget. I have an interview for a new job tomorrow night so I won't be able to make it home for dinner.

Monica's Father – A new job huh? What is it?

Monica – I don't wanna really say until I actually get it.

Monica's Father – Well, you're an adult. You're free to tell me whenever you're ready though. Dinner will be set in about ten minutes.

-Monica's father then walks away as Monica begins to softly talk to herself.

Monica – Actually, it's a job that might make my life perfect again.

Scene 4

-In the elementary school cafeteria Monica sits next to Sami who is drawing a picture.

Sami – Look Miss Monica. I made a picture of a ninja who can shoot rainbow lightning that turns people into cans of cola!

Monica – Wow Sami. That's just... wow.

-From nearby, Madison walks over to Monica with a small colorful pot holder in her hand. As soon as Madison reaches Monica, Madison hands Monica the pot holder.

Monica – Hey Madison. Is this something you want me to look at?

Madison – I made it. You can keep it.

Monica – Thank you Madison. Wow. Look at the level of detail in this thing. Plus it feels very thick. I could actually use this in the kitchen.

Sami – That's so cool looking. I bet you could use it to hand ice cream over to aliens.

Monica – Hold on. What?

-Suddenly the three are interrupted by the voice of Sami's mother who has just entered the room.

Sami's Mother – Sami. It's time to go home.

Sami – Okay mom! Bye Miss Monica!

-Sami instantly begins to walk away as Monica turns her head a bit as she smiles.

Monica – Madison. You live in the same neighborhood as Sami right?

Madison – Yeah.

Monica – So... has she always been so crazy?

Madison – Not always. When she was in kindergarten, she was very quiet.

Monica – So when did Sami start acting so... Sami?

Madison – When you started working here and started laughing at her jokes and drawings.

Monica – Wow. So...

Madison – Hey. Do you want to play a card game with me?

Monica – Oh, I'm sorry Madison. But I'm going to be leaving a little early today. I got permission to go to a job interview.

Madison – You're leaving us for another job?

Monica – Well it's an interview. Nothing is certain. If I do leave though, I will miss getting awesome new pictures from you. By the way Madison, before I forget to ask you: when *did* you start making lots of great art all of the time?

Madison – Well when I first met... Oh. I see my dad coming outside. I guess I'm going home early. Bye Miss Monica.

-Madison suddenly wraps her arms around Monica, hugging her for a moment. Monica simply accepts the hug looking slightly caught off guard. Madison lets go and then runs over to her father who has just walked into the room. Monica just watches Madison walk away. As Monica watches, she begins to smile.

Scene 5

-Monica walks down a sidewalk with a small piece of paper in her hand. Monica glances at the paper and then at a small office building to her right.

Monica – Well, this is the address he gave me.

-Monica walks over to the door of the small office building. She opens the door to see a large empty room with nothing but several empty chairs and three individuals standing in the middle of the room: Charles, and two more men wearing black suits.

Charles – Hello Miss Daves. I'm pleased to see that you took me up on my offer to meet and discuss your future. Won't you please take a seat?

Monica – You know when you said that we'd be meeting at an undercover building, I didn't expect an abandoned office building. Kinda creepy if you think about it.

Charles – Hence, an undercover building. Now won't you please take a seat?

Monica – I thought this was gonna be a one on one interview. Why do we need the men in black to stand and watch us?

Charles – Again, won't you please take a seat?

Monica - You know I think I'm gonna need a lot more legit proof before I start talking to you about anything. I mean you may have a decent ID but the methods you came up with to speak with me don't seem to line up right.

Charles – Miss Daves, won't you please take a seat?

Monica – And now that I think about it, I spent my last year of high school working for the best lawyers in this state, and they gave me a lot of inside know how on how the FBI works, and nothing I'm seeing from you guys seems to match up with the reality of how the FBI really works. So what's really going on here?

-Suddenly the two black suited men rush forward and push Monica into a chair. The two men then hold her down in the chair tightly as Monica struggles to get free.

Charles – I told you to sit down.

Monica – What the heck are you doing to me? You're not FBI agents!

Charles – Oh but we are Miss Daves. But we've recently chosen to take up employment with different parties. In fact, our benefactor would like to meet you now.

-Charles turns his head towards a nearby door.

Charles – You can come in Mr. Blaze.

-From the nearby door, a blond haired man in a black suit named Blaze comes in.

Blaze – Hello Miss Daves. Welcome to the perfect life.

Scene 6

-Monica sits strapped to a metal chair with metal constraints on her arms and legs. Attached to the chair is a large machine full of many wires and circuits. Monica turns her head to see Charles, Blaze, and the two black suited men watching her.

Monica – So what kind of game are you jerks playing? And who are you supposed to be mister big boss man?

Blaze – I am but a humble servant of a country that is enemy of this one. My leaders have been infiltrating your land for the last several years searching for methods to obtain power from within this nation. We came close to obtaining powerful technology some time ago through a clone that attempted to act as a boy's future daughter. However that effort resulted in failure. But, rather than attempt to manipulate the minds of those that would be our enemies, we have decided now to simply take control of them.

Monica – You know blabbing your whole evil plan to somebody always results in negative consequences later down the road.

Blaze – Not if you become one of us.

Monica – Ooo. Are we talking hypnosis or mental torture? You picked the wrong lady to abduct you sickos. I've got the strongest mind you've ever come across.

Blaze – We are quite aware of your high intellect Miss Daves. Which is why we have chosen to possess you.

Monica – What the heck do you mean by possess?

Blaze – Agent Charles and his allies believe that they willingly joined my cause. When in reality, it is the technology that my home land recently acquired that allowed their wills to bend to mine so easily.

Monica – So you put them under mind control then?

Blaze – Oh but the technology I have that is used to possess individuals is so much more than just mind control. Wouldn't you like to know how it works?

-Monica sits silently and still.

Blaze – When the machine you see next to you is activated, it forces any individual connected to it to dream of their greatest desires. As they drift deeper into their fantasy though, the machine begins to attach itself to the person's fantasy. Then when the individual completely accepts their fantasy and their soul is disconnected with reality, the catch is made. The person suddenly finds themselves accepting my will as if it is their greatest desire, and that person shall be possessed for the rest of their days.

-Monica's face suddenly becomes one of fear. She instantly begins to struggle to get out of her confinement.

Monica – Ugg. Err. Let me out! You can't control me!

-Blaze begins to walk over to the nearby machine as he glances back at Monica.

Blaze – What's the matter Miss Daves? Do you have a perfect life you dream of and desire so much that you're worried it really would take a hold of your mind? Excellent.

-Monica's face becomes incredibly worried.

Monica – No! Please no!!!

-Blaze then presses a large button on the machine.

Blaze – Prepare to enter your perfect life now Miss Daves.

-Suddenly the machine glows as does Monica's body. Monica begins to look up as everything begins to look bright in her eyes.

Monica – Nooooooo!

Scene 7

-In a small bedroom, a twenty two year old woman named Monica slowly opens her eyes as she glances at the bed she is laying in. Monica begins to shake her head a bit as she gets up and speaks softly to herself.

Monica *– Man. What a crazy dream.*

-Monica looks in a mirror briefly to make sure her attire looks appropriate and then walks out of her room and towards the kitchen. As soon as she enters the kitchen, she sees her father and mother both already sitting at the kitchen table eating breakfast. Monica's two parents both instantly see her walking into the kitchen.

Monica's Mother – Well look who finally woke up. My daughter: the valedictorian, and queen of bed hair.

-Monica begins to roll her eyes as she sits with her parents.

Monica – Ha, ha mom. Very funny.

Monica's Mother – Stay right there. I need to find a camera and take a picture of this. The days of us seeing you with bed hair may never happen again once you start working at that new law firm that just hired you and you move out of here.

-Monica's father looks at his watch and suddenly begins to get up.

Monica's Father – Oops. I'm gonna be late. I have to head to the office.

Monica's Mother – Honestly dear. You're the mayor. The man running this town. Who are you going to get in trouble with?

-Monica's father grabs a suitcase and heads towards the door but quickly stops. He heads back over towards Monica and looks at her.

Monica's Father – Good luck at your graduation rehearsal today. I know the real one is this weekend but... I just wanted to tell you how proud I am of you making it this far.

Monica – Hey. College wasn't that hard. In fact it was one of the best times of my life. But I seriously couldn't have made it if it wasn't for you guys.

-Monica's mother and father instantly both hug her.

Monica's Mother – We both love you so much Monica and we're so proud of you.

Monica – I'm just lucky to have two great parents like you guys.

Scene 8

-*Monica walks down a sidewalk with a smile on her face while from nearby a blond haired woman in a long red dress walks over to Monica. Monica quickly glances at the woman.*

Monica – *Well if it isn't Trina Jackson of the Simple Town Gazette. What new quotes are you trying to get out of me today?*

-*The woman: Trina smirks as she begins to walk right next to Monica.*

Trina – *Monica Daves, you've solidified yourself as one of the most intelligent young minds in the fields of law. Your papers, research, and aide you've given several big name law firms over the last four years have mesmerized countless individuals. You've quickly become the greatest college student celebrity of all time. However, people want to hear the simple human angle today. They want to know what Monica Daves is feeling on the verge of her graduation from law school.*

Monica – *Just that... I made it and I know I've got a great future ahead of me! Life is as perfect as it gets right now.*

-*Monica looks down and suddenly she realizes she's about to bump into Madison and Sami who are drawing with chalk on the sidewalk.*

Monica – *Whoa. Look out!*

-*Monica and Trina both stop walking as both Madison and Sami look up at the two.*

Monica – *Sorry we almost bumped into your girls. Hey. Are your parents nearby?*

Madison – *We live on this street. Both of our parents are watching us from the windows.*

Monica – *You both live on this street? Wow. I've been walking on this sidewalk to get to the building a bunch of my classes are in for years and I've never seen you two before.*

Sami – *Hey, um... do you... uh... do you...*

Monica – *Do I what?*

Madison – *She's quiet sometimes because she's worried people will think she's weird. I think she was gonna ask if you wanted to draw pictures with us.*

Monica – *Sorry but I'm busy doing more important things right now. Bye.*

-Monica then begins to walk away from Madison and Sami but then instantly she freezes. Suddenly everything around Monica begins to disappear. Tears begin to appear in Monica's eyes as she begins to scream.

Monica - Nnnnnnnoooooooo!!!!!

-Sparks begin to fly out of the machine connected to Monica as Blaze, Charles, and the other two men back away from it.

Charles – I thought you said that machine was full proof.

Blaze – It was. It should've showed her...

-Suddenly tons of sparks and wind began to shoot out of the machine as Monica screams.

Monica - Nnnnnnnoooooooo!!!!!

-The machine and the entire room begin to shake. The shaking causes the metal constraints to break loose from the chair Monica is in. Monica quickly jumps out of her chair. Monica takes a step forward but suddenly she realizes her body is very weak. Monica then falls to the ground as the men stand confused.

Blaze – Rrr. How dare my plan fail? We must take her with us before...

-Suddenly several army soldiers run into the room with their guns pointed at the men. The lead soldier smirks as he takes a close look at the men's faces.

Lead Soldier – Hello Mr. Blaze. There are a lot of people in Washington that have been trying to put a stop to you and your unique brand of terrorism. Keep your arms where I can see them and no funny moves.

-Another soldier goes over to Monica and helps her up.

Solider – Are you okay ma'am?

Monica – I'm okay. Actually... things are more okay than I thought they were.

Scene 9

-In the elementary school cafeteria Monica sits with Madison and Sami. The three are drawing pictures together as they talk at the same time.

Sami – And then I told the class about how when I become a scientist, I'm gonna make all kinds of cool gadgets and weapons for ninjas to use to stop the samurai bunnies from Canada.

-Monica begins to laugh at Sami but then stops as she begins to talk.

Monica – So what did your teacher say when she heard you say this?

Sami – She just looked at me and said – I hope you're not disappointed if you don't get that kind of job one day.

Madison – I know what she kind of means. My teacher told me that when you're an adult, you don't always get your first choice of the kind of job or life you want. That's why if I don't get to be a marine biologist, I know I could always try instead to be a vet or a zoo keeper. In fact, I might even like those jobs even more.

Monica – Yeah, you never know.

Sami – Hey Miss Monica. Did you get to do the kind of job you wanted to do when you were young?

Monica – To be honest guys, no. This isn't the kind of life I thought I'd be living when I was young. This isn't what I dreamed a perfect life for me would look like.

Madison – Well what kind of perfect life did you dream about when you were young?

Monica – Well interesting that you ask. I actually sort of… had that dream again yesterday. I dreamed of a life where everything that I wanted to see happen when I was younger actually happened. I was in my bed and walked into the kitchen to see my perfect family. Then I walked out the door of my house and realized that I was popular and was practically like a celebrity. It was everything that I had ever wanted.

Madison – And then what happened?

Monica – Well I was walking down the sidewalk and then I saw…

-Monica pauses for a moment and looks at both Madison and Sami.

Monica - ...the most horrible thing ever. Then I snapped back to reality and realized that my real life right now may not be perfect, but it's actually pretty...

Sami – Hey I see my mom coming from the window.

Madison – Yeah, and there's my dad. Bye Miss Monica.

Sami – Bye Miss Monica.

-Madison and Sami both begin to get up but then Monica holds out her hand and speaks to them.

Monica – Hold on girls. Wait.

-Monica then instantly rushes towards the two girls and hugs them. The two girls stand slightly confused as Monica hugs them.

Madison – What's this for?

Monica – For helping me see that I have the best life ever.

THE END

Chapter 10 – The Undesired Outcome

Keno McFly

Update Info   View Activity Log •••

Timeline   About   Friends 396   Photos   More ▾

The Beginning of Adulthood, By Keno McFly: Age 18

Hey everyone out there in cyberspace. It's your friend Keno. I'm starting college next week, and in many respects: beginning adulthood as well. To help keep people in the know of what I'm up to, I thought it would be interesting if from time to time, I sent you all some notes about what I'm up to in the wide world of college. For those interested in what I'll be studying in college, here's the low down. After spending several years as a volunteer at the "Tree of Life After School Care Club", I've decided to pursue a career in teaching children. Thus, I've declared my major in "Education". One of the best things about the particular college I'm going to is that they rush all college students into public school internships as soon as possible, so I'll be getting a chance to feel like a real teacher sooner than later. So if all goes according to plan, I'll have a great four years of college classes and internships, and be a public school teacher by age 22. Here's to a great future. Talk to you all later!

My Future is Unknown, By Keno McFly: Age 19

For the last several years of my life I thought I was sure on what I wanted to do with my life, which was to be a public school teacher. However things are getting complicated with that vision because my life is changing.

For the last four months I have been a college intern in an elementary school. I was taking college courses half the week and helping teach elementary school students the other half. However things just haven't felt right. I internally felt a great loss from not being able to teach children the themes I could teach at church or other organizations with good values I've worked over the years for such as the "Tree of Growth" after care. I knew it was going to come with the territory of being a public school teacher but what I didn't expect was feeling like a core piece of who I was would be yanked away. But is it the right choice?

So now I face the realization that my future is unknown due to the fact that I have some big choices ahead of me. Do I choose to continue working in the public schools? Do I choose to work in some type of after school program full time? Do I work in something not even related to what I am not even considering right now? These thoughts have been messing with my heads for months now.

The reasoning behind my consideration for working in the public schools is this. Without going into details (for the sake of professionalism), I am just shocked and distressed at the way too many public school teachers think of students. For example, one too many teachers I've seen just let rude comments students say to one another just slip by. They're just letting students bully each other and say rude things to one another on a constant basis (and I'm not talking little things here). So do I become a public school teacher in order to teach children the appropriate way to treat one another while having to still support the teachers that don't share these simple but important values?

A part of me is also considering external factors that may be affecting this decision. Am I simply yearning for the comfort that church and my old after care job naturally give me? Am I trying to find escape from the pressure the university and public school system is putting on me? If I do take on another job, will I have to go back and take a lot more college classes before I graduate? What about being in an insecure financial situation? It's a real mix of emotions.

So if anyone that actually read this whole thing could please keep me in their prayers, that would be great. And if you have your own opinion/suggestion on my situation, feel free to comment or send me a message via inbox. And if you did read this whole thing, thank you reading.

Future Career Unknown, By Keno McFly: Age 20

So it's been a strange day and mind-shaking year for me so far. For those that already read my note that I made last year, then you would know that I have already been struggling on what I want to do with my future. I originally had my mind set on being a teacher long ago but for a year now have been having second thoughts about that field.

Anyway over the last two years without sounding too prideful, I have become much better with creating lessons plans and designing curriculum that teach important life lessons and social skills that I've been able to give and even sell to churches and multiple after school care organizations. Meanwhile ever since my newest internship in the public school began during the fall, it's been one mistake and one trial after another. Yes, I know it's challenging for all but it became clearly evident that I was not meeting the standards that all of the other interns around me were supposed to be meeting.

So anyway to keep it short and simple, I was told today that I wasn't meeting the requirements of the internship position and would have to be dismissed. Now on a positive note, I was told that I had constantly used and attempted to implement all advice/suggestions given to me, and that I had made progress. However the rate was undesirable. So now on Monday morning I am going to meet with several university people to talk about what I'm doing next and so on. I am already told I will be able to have a few additional days to have closure with my mentor and the students, but I will not be passing the 15-credit worth internship. Basically, I failed at being an intern.

Now it would sound like this ordeal might have me depressed but for some reason I can't explain, I'm not. I had been putting consideration into doing some type of career that could put my beliefs into action, and now I feel like I can.

I will say that I don't feel like this current semester has been a waste. I have had the best and most supportive mentor in the world, and through her example I have learned so much in how to treat fellow staff members, how to talk to parents, and how to have a better outlook at working with children. All of these are things that I can transfer to other job placements. In fact, I look forward to using some of the information I have used through the school system in other jobs I have in the future.

Anyway as some say, when one door closes, another one opens. The nice thing is I feel like another door has already been opened. It's just taking the closing of this current one before me to realize it. The problem is I don't know where this other door is or where it will be taking me.

So I'm just sending this message out there for any prayer or support of any kind I could get. Again, I will be having some meeting on Monday with a bunch of university people that may potentially show me options of things I can do, like what kind of major I can switch into. Until then, we'll just see what the Lord has in store for me.

Trying to Figure Out Future Career, By Keno McFly: Age 21

Today I received several college class assignments that operate on the assumption that the student (me) has already picked a specific future career already. The problem is I'm still trying to figure it out. I mean, even though I switched my major from "Education" to "Family Science", there's still a lot of possibilities in what I should investigate. Over the last year I have narrowed down my list of potential options (such as not becoming a public school teacher now), but I still feel too undecided. The only potential ideas I've got so far are: after school child care leader, professional developer of children's education curriculum, government social worker, or family counselor.

These are the ideas that have floated through my head recently but I'm also open to the idea of taking on something else if it seems right. While I haven't tried to have this choice mess with my head over the last few months, I will need to make some kind of choice soon. For one, I need to do a big research project soon into my potential future career. Two, I will need to soon set up my final semester of college internship which can be in any type of field the university believes has a strong link to Family Science (FYI, it has the be in a job environment I haven't worked in before), and I would like to intern in the actual job that I want a career in. I do know that plans can change even after you've gotten a degree. I also know that the good Lord is leading me to something special even though I don't know what it is.

Anyway, I made this note for three reasons. One: to get my thoughts out in the open. Two: to share a prayer concern (FYI: I will be talking with a career counselor in the Family Science department on Thursday so prayers on that would be good). Three: to hear anyone's thoughts or opinions on what I should do. Crunch time is coming close for me, and I at least need to have a temporary career goal in the near future.

A Positive Joyful Spirit Always, By Keno McFly: Age 22

So ever since I graduated from college a few months ago, I've been looking to find a job... and I haven't found any. It's been really difficult facing rejection after rejection. However: as important as getting a job is to one's life, an important lesson I've had to learn recently though is that... my life right now isn't so bad. I mean for the last several months, I've been struggling to get full time work because well – that's what you're supposed to do after you graduate from college. Duh! But while on that journey I sort of bought into the idea that I think a lot of people have, which is... once you have a job, everything will be good and you will feel fulfilled.

The thing is, while a job is necessary to have while on this world, a job alone isn't going to make you feel completely fulfilled. That can only come from dedicating one's life to God. Let me back up and put this in perspective. At many stages of our life, we feel like once we get some "thing", everything is going to be better. Some young children think that if they get a new toy or game, their life will be complete. Some teenagers think that if they get the latest cell phone or electronic device, they will at last fit in with their peers. Some young adults think if they can get married as soon as possible, that all of their problems will go away. Some parents think that as soon as they get their children into a new "special" school or get that one new "special" service, that everything related to their child's grades and behavior will improve. And yes, many adults out there (including myself for a while) feel that getting a full time job, will make everything better.

The thing is, obtaining some "thing" of this world, isn't going to make everything better, at least not forever. Obtaining new toys and gadgets isn't going to help for too long since they'll eventually become outdated or boring. Getting married just to get away from problems, seems like it would create more problems (or so I hear since I wouldn't know from personal experience). Assuming a "special" new service will eliminate all problems is ridiculous since there is no such thing as one service that eliminates all problems.

We constantly think that getting a "thing" of this world will make everything better. But getting a "thing", isn't going to help us in eternity. We can't revolve our joyful spirits completely around what we have and don't have, whether they be things or even job statuses. We can't determine how much we worship and thank the Lord based on if we think He has given us a lot or not a lot recently. Rather our level of joy and worship should remain constant because God will always love us, he has done a ton for us, and he's still doing so much for us. I mean not only has the Lord given me food, air, shelter, friends, and all that good stuff... he's made sure I've always had just enough money to make it by each month, a great house renting arrangement that doesn't cost me too much, a car that's still got a couple of years more life in it, and really good health. Plus a job counselor I talked to recently looked at the numbers, and said even though I don't have a full time job right now, the percentage of people who call me back after I send them a job resume and cover letter, is actually much higher than what the average job seeker gets. So apparently I'm doing something right, and statistically speaking: I have a much better chance to find a job soon versus the average job seeker.

So what I have I discovered lately in nutshell? Well, I can't live my life under the assumption that once I get a job or get that one little improvement in my life, that everything will be better. Because in reality, that may not be true.

Also, it's important to not just say the future won't be so bad; rather one should also say, the present isn't so bad either. And more importantly, I can't revolve my joyful spirit and worship around whether I have a job or not. Jobs are things that come and go in this world. But God and the amazing things he does will always be there. So I'm gonna maintain a positive joyful attitude before and after I get that future job one day (always). And more importantly I'm going to remember what Jeremiah 29: 11 in the good book says – "For I know the plans I have for you," declares the Lord, "plans to prosper you and not to harm you, plans to give you hope and a future."

The Next Step, By Keno McFly: Age 23

So life has been interesting. While struggling to get by with various part time and odd jobs, I had a run in with my old friend from high school: Monica Daves. After a positive reputation she obtained by running an after school care club in a county run organization, she's planning to start her own after care organization but is looking for the right place to run it. I then immediately told her of the old after care I used to work at. We both soon learned that the building that housed it is available to rent and all of the old supplies are still present in the building.

So after a lot of talk and preparing, it's official: this fall I am going to be the assistant of the new and improved "Tree of Life After School Care Club". So far, me and Monica's plans include having lots of art activities, both indoor and outdoor sports activities, and a fair amount of time set aside to just talk with the students in order to build positive relationships with them and teach them important life lessons.

It's funny how back when I started college, this wasn't my original plan. However, I can't think of any better outcome for my life than where I am now. Here's to a great future. Talk to you all later!

THE END

What Happens Next to Keno, Jimmy, Kaitlyn and Monica? Find Out in the Sequel Novel:

<u>Bonus Page – Original Cover Sketches</u>

About the Author

"Captain Sean" is an experienced children's leader from Silver Spring, Maryland with over a decade's worth of experience teaching children and teens in public school and church settings. He is an award winning story teller who is dedicated to creating stories that teach relevant themes and values through creative means for young people as a way to help inspire them to become amazing adults.

Made in the USA
Middletown, DE
10 May 2015